'Powerful, intelligent and moving, a very assured and intricately plotted debut novel, with a great sense of place.'

Graeme Simsion
Author of *The Rosie Project* and *The Rosie Effect*

'Susan Gandar's story bridges different times, different worlds, with energy, drive and elegance. She writes with a sense of subtle wonder that her characters share with the reader, but the real mystery, as in all good storytelling, is timeless; how we live, how we love, and above all who we really are. A great read.'

Michael Russell
Author of *The City of Shadows* and *The City of Strangers*

'Couldn't put it down.'

Clara Salaman
Author of *Shame on You* and *The Boat*

D0813143

we've come to take you HOME

SUSAN GANDAR

Matador
9 Priory Business Park,
Wistow Road, Kibworth Beauchamp,
Leicestershire. LE8 0RX
Tel: 0116 279 2299
Email: books@troubador.co.uk
Web: www.troubador.co.uk/matador
Twitter: @matadorbooks

ISBN 978 1785890 406

British Library Cataloguing in Publication Data.
A catalogue record for this book is available from the British Library.

Printed and bound in the UK by TJ International, Padstow, Cornwall
Typeset in 11pt Aldine401 BT by Troubador Publishing Ltd, Leicester, UK

Matador is an imprint of Troubador Publishing Ltd

To Alice and Olivia

There was a long, drawn-out sigh, followed by the tearing of the air, and the surrounding darkness was split by a flash of white light. Sam expected to see the lights on the promenade twinkling off into the distance, the wings of the angel statue silhouetted against the moonlit sky, the cliffs standing sentinel at either end of the town. But what she expected no longer existed.

Stretching out ahead was a vast wasteland; a filthy, oozing sea of mud studded with the blackened stumps of lifeless trees. Craters, filled with slimy water, touched and overlapped all the way to the horizon. Beaten down into this mess were scraps of equipment, helmets, rifles, coils of barbed wire, even a military tank.

A gold ring, embedded in a piece of rock, lay beside her feet. She looked more closely. The piece of rock wasn't rock but a human finger. As she looked even more closely, the finger connected itself to a hand, a hand attached itself to an arm, a head stuck itself onto a neck, the neck onto a back with two shoulders. The bones jerked and a rat, as big as a cat, tore itself out of the ribcage of a man who used to be somebody's husband.

The sea of mud wasn't that at all. It was a sea of blood and bones. There were arms, legs, heads and hands, some still wearing clothes, some still with eyes and hair, layer upon layer of them. And the blood and the bones weren't all dead. Some were still alive and still suffering. Their cries rose up all around her.

A head lifted out of the mud. A pair of blue eyes blinked. And blinked again.

'Jess...'

A hand reached out towards her.

'Jess...'

ONE

IF THE FOUR OF them had been entered into a competition to see who could scream the longest and the loudest there would have been no contest; Shelly would easily be 'Outstanding Screamer of the Year'.

They'd been on the Orbiter, the Freak Out, the Booster, and now it was the turn of the Tagada. They were sitting, side by side, on the slippery plastic bench, their arms hooked over the bar behind their backs, while the giant bowl spun round and round, and up and down, faster and faster. Up and round, down and round it went, with Shelly screaming her head off, Lou moaning on and on about feeling sick and Katie shouting out lists of instructions nobody could hear.

Round it went again, and looking up at them, laughing and waving, were four faces. Male ones. And Katie and Shelly and Lou were laughing and trying to wave back while keeping one arm hooked over the bar. So these were the boys. And which of the four was the one who wanted so much to meet her?

Was it the very tall one in the Hawaiian shirt; the very short, stocky one who kept punching the air; the one wearing dark glasses even though the sun had gone down over an hour ago; or the very thin, pale, freckly one with red hair. The ride was slowing down. It stopped.

The thought of going out, being kissed, perhaps even going to bed with any of the knock-kneed, spotty-faced male specimens, dribbling the ball up and down the school's football field, was just too hideous. But Shelly had been there, done it and survived. Although the great love affair to end all love affairs had lasted less than four weeks.

'Guys...'

And Katie was throwing herself at the very tall one. Shelly had her arms locked round the waist of the short, stocky one. And Lou was nibbling at the neck of the one in the dark glasses. His face, the little that Sam could see of it, was the sort of grey that comes from staring at computer screens for twenty hours a day.

'I'm Leo...'

She hated red hair almost as much as she hated freckles.

'Hi, I'm Sam.'

The ghost train siren wailed. There was a crash, a shriek, and then the first cab, with Lou sitting beside the boy in the dark glasses, skidded down the slope towards a set of double doors.

'Who's he?'

Katie and the boy in the Hawaiian shirt were draped around each other in the cab directly ahead.

'That's Josh...'

The boy in the Hawaiian shirt took a swig from a bottle.

'He wants to be a doctor. At least that's what he tells the girls...'

The cab rolled down the slope towards the double doors.

'Girls like Katie?'

Their own cab juddered forward. Leo put his arm around her.

'Yep, you've got it, girls like Katie...'

The doors slammed open and they were hurtling through a narrow tunnel with black ceiling and walls. A skeleton with glowing red eyes lunged down. Sam shrieked. Leo laughed and pulled her towards him, tightening his arm around her shoulder.

The cab careered round a corner and through another set

of doors. If it had been dark before then this was really dark. There was rattle of iron followed by a wail and a shrouded figure clanked out of an alcove. Cobwebs brushed across Sam's face. Through another set of doors and in front of them, dangling from the roof, was a cage. Inside, its hands and feet bound in chains, was a decomposing body of a man. The corpse raised its head, rolled its eyes and grinned. Round another corner, and now they were plunging down a slope and through another set of double doors.

Moonlight, silence and a flickering sky replaced the crashing and banging and wailing of the ghost train. She was no longer sitting beside Leo. She was standing on the platform of a station. Carriages, the old-fashioned kind she'd seen in black and white films, with red crosses painted on their sides, stretched down the platform ahead of her.

Men in military uniform and women, wearing ankle-length dresses and long white aprons, red and grey capes draped over their shoulders, walked up and down, whispering instructions; one stretcher was directed here, another there, another was loaded onto a truck parked at the side of the platform. There must have been hundreds of them.

A young woman, wearing a blouse, skirt and coat rather than a nurse's uniform, was walking down the platform towards her. Head down, looking from side to side, she checked each stretcher, before moving on, down the row, to the next, and the next. There was a cry. The woman walked on. The cry was repeated. The woman stopped. She turned.

TWO

August 1914

'THERE WERE NO ANGELS.'

'The soldiers saw them at Mons. The newspaper said so–'

Her mother couldn't read.

'Newspaper? What newspaper?'

But neither could her father.

'At the grocers, in the window, Jess read it out for me...'

Today was Saturday and on a Saturday her father always got back from work early enough for the family to have tea together.

'Five days of marching with no sleep? Of course they were seeing angels. So would you, Mother, so would I, so would Jess, all dressed in white, with wings, sitting on horses... '

Along paths, up lanes and over hills, he would always find a perfect place for a picnic. Today they were sitting beside the river, in a meadow, just a short walk from the cottage.

'And the swords...'

'Swords? What swords?'

'The angels were carrying swords...'

Jess took a bite. The bread was warm, the cheese tangy, the pickled onion crunchy.

'All big and flaming...'

A whistle echoed from further down the valley. Jess jumped up. She ran across the meadow and leapt up the steps, two at a time, onto the narrow, wooden bridge. To her left, the river tumbled down a weir while, to her right, it flowed, slow and smooth, towards the sea.

4

A belch of black smoke, another whistle, the grind and rattle of metal on metal, and the train was thundering past. She waved and waved until her arm ached. It wouldn't be long before she was a giggling servant girl, with a job in the big city and money in her pocket, on her way down for a bit of fun at the seaside.

But there were no plump-cheeked, giggling servant girls hanging out of the windows. Not a single one. Soldiers now stood, squeezed together, shoulder to shoulder, along the length of the train. They didn't see her standing there on the bridge waving. Or if they did, they didn't nod, smile or raise a hand.

'They're off to France. To fight for king and country.'

She had to ask her father the question. Even if the answer was the one she was most dreading.

'Will you have to do your duty?'

"England expects that every man will do his duty" had been the headline, the day war was declared.

'Will you have to go to France?'

A thump, thump, thump of drums was followed by the blare of trumpets.

'It's a band...'

Her mother was packing up the picnic.

'Like at the seaside...'

The sound of cheering drifted across the meadow.

'Don't want to miss it.'

The four of them, Jess running ahead, her father and then her mother, carrying her baby brother, followed the path across the meadow, through the rickety iron gate and up the steep lane, lined on either side with stone cottages. They joined the other men, women and children walking towards a platform draped with red, white and blue bunting.

'Are you, you and you...'

The band fell silent.

5

'Are you really satisfied with what you are doing today? Do you feel happy as you walk along the streets and see other men wearing the King's uniform?'

A man was standing on the platform. He was dressed in a suit, with a neat moustache and slicked back hair. A line of soldiers, sweating in tightly buttoned khaki, stood below him.

'What will you say in years to come when people ask, "Where did you serve in the Great War?"'

In a country she'd never heard of, hundreds of miles away, somebody who was not at all important had shot somebody very important. A country had invaded another country, a different country had invaded another country, and so it had gone on, until it seemed that the whole world was at war.

'What will you answer when your children grow up and say, "Father, why weren't you a soldier too?"'

And now this Great War had arrived in her village.

'Who made this little island the greatest and most powerful Empire the world has ever seen?'

The man opened his arms.

'Your forefathers.'

There was a cheer from the front of the crowd.

'Who ruled this Empire with such wisdom and sympathy that every part of it, of whatever race or origin, has rallied to it in its hour of need?'

A young man raised his hand.

'Our fathers.'

It was Robert Tucker, the vicar's son. He had visited their cottage when her mother had been taken ill. He had come over to where Jess was sitting, hunched in a corner. He knelt down beside her, took her hand, held it tight and told her, promised her, that there was no need to be frightened. And he'd been right. Her mother had recovered.

Another hand was raised.

'Our fathers.'

6

'That's Dr. Crow's boy, isn't it? Thought he was going into his father's practice…'

'Not now, he won't, Mother.'

A soldier guided the two young men over to a table where another soldier was waiting.

'Who will stand up to preserve this great and glorious heritage?'

The man on the platform looked down at Norman Smith and Dick Butler.

'Lads?'

They raised their hands.

'We will.'

Stan Booth raised his hand.

'I will.'

The man on the platform pointed down at the three of them: Norman, who could score a goal from any angle; Dick, who had kissed every girl in the village; and Stan, the gentle giant who always gave Jess a bunch of flowers, freshly picked from the hedgerow, on her birthday.

'You will.'

Three soldiers walked towards the three boys. Jess' father pushed through the crowd.

'Stan, your parents, what about the farm?'

'The harvest's in.'

Stan was always happy.

'Your parents?'

Nothing that anyone said or did could ever stop him smiling.

'I'll be back by Christmas.'

And it was the same now.

'They need you–'

A soldier held her father back.

'Leave the lad alone. He can make up his own mind.'

'He's not eighteen.'

'Looks old enough to me.'

The soldiers, going out to fight in France, were no longer strangers, standing shoulder to shoulder, on a passing train. They were the men who lived in her village; the boys she'd gone to school with, grown up with.

'Justify the faith of your fathers.'

The man on the platform smiled down at her.

'Earn the gratitude of your children.'

She grabbed hold of her father's arm.

'You can't go. I don't want you to go.'

He squeezed her hand.

'We've all got to do our duty.'

A soldier was walking towards them.

'He's too old, my father's too old…'

She'd read it in the newspaper.

'He's thirty-…'

She had to remember.

'Thirty-six, my father's thirty-six.'

'Come on, lass. Let him go.'

'She's right. My daughter's right. My husband was thirty-six,' her mother spat the words out, 'four months ago.'

The soldier released her father's arm.

There was a thump, followed by a blare and the crowd cheered as the boys, heads held high, arms swinging, marched down the main street. The conquering heroes, their war won, would be home in time for Christmas. Beer was drunk, flowers were thrown and the National Anthem was sung, again and again.

THREE

A YOUNG MAN WAS struggling to sit up. Or what was left of a young man. Where there should have been an arm and a hand with five fingers there was splintered bone. Where there should have been a leg and a foot with five toes there was a stump. On the right side of his head, instead of an ear and eye, there was a gaping hole.

'Sam, Sam, can you hear me? Are you OK?'

She opened her eyes. No station, no platform, no young man with a hole for a face.

'You went all cold, like ice, and then you started screaming, really screaming...'

She was at the fairground, sitting beside Leo in the cab of the ghost train.

'I saw...'

She didn't want to go there.

'Nothing. It was nothing...'

'Nothing? You must have seen something to make you scream that loud.'

'It was the body, the one in the cage...'

The siren began to wail.

'You're lying, Sam Foster.'

The cab juddered.

'It wasn't that lump of old plastic with the rolling eyes that spooked you...'

Leo took her hand.

'So what now, the Superbowl? Or the Sky Dancer?'

Katie was still entwined around the boy in the Hawaiian shirt. Lou was nibbling at the neck of the boy in the dark glasses. And somewhere, on the other side of the fairground, Shelly was screaming.

'I'm sorry, Leo...'

It wasn't the freckles.

'Sorry?'

It wasn't the red hair.

'You're really nice...'

He let go of her hand.

'But?'

Better to tell the truth.

'I want to go home.'

He stared at her long and hard.

'Is it because of what happened?'

'I've told you, nothing happened.'

The train with red crosses painted along its side, the young soldier with a hole for a face, had all been as real as sitting next to Leo in the cab on the ghost train.

'Something did happen, Sam, when we were in that tunnel.'

He stepped towards her.

'I couldn't see it, couldn't hear it, but if one day you want to tell someone—'

She pushed him away.

'Leo. I'm fine. Stop worrying about me, go and join the others. Have some fun...'

'At least let me walk you home. We could stop off and—'

'No, please, I'll be fine.'

'You're sure?'

'I'm sure.'

'Really sure?'

'Really, really sure.'

'OK.'

He still didn't move.

'What shall I tell them? The others?'

'The usual, anything – that I saw a ghost and got freaked out – now go on, please.'

She walked away from the noise of the fairground, following the lights twinkling along the seafront. A few hours ago, she'd been standing at her bedroom window watching as the waves hurled themselves up against the promenade wall. The battering went on and on, each surge stronger than the last, but the concrete slabs of the wall had held and the sea had been contained. Now the tide was turning and the sea was retreating but it was going reluctantly, sucking in, dragging down, everything in its path.

Rain, first one spot, then another, spat down from above. A young man, dressed in military uniform, khaki tunic and breeches, knee-high leather boots, a wide belt with a strap going over his right shoulder, turned and smiled as she passed the angel statue.

There had been a photograph on the front page of the newspaper a couple of days ago. It was of four soldiers, standing together in a group, dressed in full combat gear, looking directly at the camera. She couldn't remember where the photograph had been taken, whether it was somewhere in the Middle East, in the Far East or in Africa. But she would never forget those faces looking out at her. Minutes later one of those soldiers was dead, shot through the head by an enemy sniper. This young man could so easily have been that young man.

She crossed the main road and turned left, then right, through the tangle of narrow alleyways leading away from the seafront. At the fork, just after the church, she started the short but steep climb out of town. Normally, even in winter, as she approached the top of the hill, she would be sweating. But tonight she was shivering.

'They wouldn't change it. It was too late.'

She pulled off her coat.

'That's what you said last year.'

Her parents were in the sitting room.

'I talked to everyone there was to talk to, pulled every string, there was nothing–'

'You treat this place like a hotel.'

The door was closed.

'It wouldn't be so bad if you were on short haul. At least you'd be at home more…'

There was something about her mother's voice, the cold, quiet, steely flatness of it.

'At least when I'm away, I'm away. Not coming and going, in and out of the house at all hours of the day and night. And you try flying backwards and forwards to Manchester three times in one day, via Dublin and Madrid and Helsinki…'

'At least I bother to remember my daughter's birthday–'

It had hurt when she was a kid, her father not being there for her birthday or for Christmas, but she'd got used to it.

'Rachel, please, don't, you know–'

'Don't what? Please don't forget who pays for all this? Was that what you were going to say?'

'No, but–'

'Well, I pay for it too, OK, not as much as you, but I work, full-time, remember, and I do all the crap stuff, the cleaning, the washing, the shopping, the cooking, the paying the bills, the going to parent-teacher meetings, that you, Mr Lord Almighty in your High And Mighty Cockpit, find too boring–'

'So, if you hate me so much what do you want me to do? Leave?'

'What an excellent idea.'

'Because if that's what you–'

'Go upstairs and pack your bags and when you go to the airport…'

12

The door slammed open.

'Don't come back.'

Her father strode out into the hallway.

'Dad?'

'Not now, Sam.'

Her father raced up the stairs two at a time. Sam peered round the sitting room door. 'Mum?'

Her mother glanced up.

'Yes?'

Sam took a step back.

'Nothing.'

The central heating was on full; her bedroom wasn't just warm, it was boiling, but she was still freezing cold. She crawled under the duvet, wearing all her clothes, her jeans, her jumper, everything, but she still couldn't stop the shivering. She stayed there for the rest of the evening, listening to the slamming of doors; her father in the main bedroom, her mother in the kitchen.

Just before ten o'clock the slamming stopped. Sam waited for a knock on the door. Her mother would come in, she would smile, even look a bit embarrassed, and say, 'Sorry about tonight, nothing to worry about, Dad's going nowhere. Now go to sleep. Everything will be fine in the morning.' There was no knock. Her mother walked straight across the landing and into the main bedroom.

That's when the talking started. Sam lay there, for two hours, listening to the rise and fall of her parents' voices. And then the talking stopped and there was silence. She pulled the duvet up over her head and closed her eyes.

There was a loud crash. Footsteps, her father's, walked down the landing and into the spare room. Something heavy was dropped on the floor. The footsteps went back along the landing and into the main bedroom.

'Don't bother coming back.'

'Don't worry I won't be.'

The door slammed shut and her father's footsteps returned along the landing, past Sam's door, into the spare room. Something else heavy was dropped on the floor.

There were more footsteps, the creak of a floorboard, and then a sound which Sam had never heard before – and which she never wanted to hear again.

She eased herself out from under the duvet, crept out of the bedroom and along the landing towards the spare room. Her father was sitting on the bed. He was crying.

'Dad...'

He wiped his eyes.

'Sam?'

He turned towards her.

'What are you doing here? Why aren't you asleep?'

'I couldn't...'

Two suitcases, large ones, were lined up just inside the open door. When her father went away flying he only ever took one.

'I've got to do what your mum's asked, Sam.'

He patted the bed. She sat down beside him.

'I don't have any choice...'

His smile was sad.

'If I refuse it will only make things worse.'

If he left, he may never come back. She had to stop him leaving.

'Mum's always saying things... getting all angry... she didn't mean–'

He raised his hand.

'She did mean it, Sam. And, I can understand why. I'm never here, always away, always flying...'

He put his arm round her.

'Whatever happens, Sam, if your mum changes her mind, even if she doesn't, you'll always have a dad, I'll always be there for you whenever you need me, we'll still see each other...'

He hugged her tight.

'OK?'

No, it wasn't, not at all, but she couldn't say it. Not here, not now.

'Now go and try and get some sleep. I'll see you in the morning.'

Lying there in her bed, her eyes wide open, Sam listened to the wind howling, the rain hammering, and the roar of the waves hurling themselves up against the beach. But the one sound she most wanted and hoped to hear was her father walking up the landing to the main bedroom, or her mother walking down the landing to the spare bedroom.

Two o'clock, three o'clock; it must have been just after four o'clock, when she finally fell asleep.

FOUR

April 1916

A BOWED FIGURE, WEARING dressing gown and pyjamas, his eyes fixed to the ground, was shambling, barefoot, towards them.

He slid his right foot forward. He tapped his toes, once, twice, at the surface of the ground. He hesitated, tapped twice again and then laid his foot down flat. He shifted his weight onto this foot and slid his left foot forward. He tapped, once, twice, at the ground and, once again, shifted his weight. He repeated this a third and fourth time and then, feet and knees together, leant over to examine the ground to his left and right. Feet still together, he examined the ground behind. He twisted back round. Back stooped, hands clenched tight, his eyes widened.

'Jess, is that…?'

His mouth opened in a silent scream.

'It can't be…'

Her mother grabbed at her arm.

'The poor boy…'

The vicar and his wife were running out of their house and down the street. The young man who had knelt down beside her, who had promised her that her mother would recover, that everything would be all right, screamed and struggled. And the more his parents fought, pulling, pushing and dragging the bent and twisted remains of their son back down the path into their house, the more he fought back.

The Battles of Le Cateau, Tannenberg, Marne, Aisne and

Ypres: the war had continued on through a second Christmas. And now, twenty months later, it was April; the military campaign, which everyone said would last for just three months, was now well into its second spring. Of the boys she had watched being cheered out of the village only a handful had returned.

The first, Dick Butler, the son of the grocer, had arrived home minus an arm and the second, Norman Smith, who used to be able to shoot a goal from any angle, minus a leg. The third, Stan Booth, whose family owned the farm where Jess' father worked as a labourer, arrived home with all his limbs but never able to walk again; a bullet in the back had left him paralysed from his waist down. The fourth, Arthur Crow, the only son of the local doctor, had been so badly burned that his own mother failed to recognise him. The trickle of wounded and disabled men had continued on and on.

Worst of all, though, was Robert Tucker, the son of the local vicar; he had been returned back to his family with all his arms and legs, completely unscarred, but his mind was gone.

'Jess, Jess, come now, there's nothing we can do. We must go home. Your father will be wanting his tea…'

Washing fluttered on the line. Daffodils nodded beside the gate. Smoke curled up out of the chimney into the sky. Her father's boots were propped up, in their usual place, on the doorstep.

'Look, Mother, your favourites. Found them down in the wood. First of the season…'

Her father placed a glass jar, crammed full with yellow primroses, down on the table. Years of working outside, hedging, ditching, mowing, ploughing, pruning, reaping and weeding, day after day, month after month, in sun, rain, wind and snow, had taken its toll.

His hands were cut and bruised. Dirt was so engrained under the broken nails that it was impossible to remove, however long and hard he scrubbed. But these hands had also gently held her hand and stroked her forehead, willing her to fight, willing her to live, when she lay, burning up with fever as a little girl, just four years old, not expected to live.

Her father took the blue and white china jug off the mantelpiece over the fireplace. There was a chink, chink, chink as he dropped in his weekly wage, coin by coin.

'Jess, what about if the two of us go and catch ourselves a couple of rabbits. Down in that dip below Horsebrook Farm beside the–'

There was a knock.

'Mr Brown?'

A boy, dressed in general post office uniform, was standing just inside the doorway.

'William Brown? William John Brown?'

'Yes.'

'For you, sir.'

The boy held out a buff-coloured envelope.

'Thank you, lad.'

The boy turned and walked away down the garden path.

'Jess, you'd best…'

She took the envelope from her father. She tore it open and unfolded the letter. She read the words, each one, slowly, to herself. Once. Twice. Her body clenched. Her mind went blank. There must be some mistake. There must be.

'Jess?'

She looked up at her father. He nodded. She swallowed. What came out was barely a whisper.

'Notice to join… the army for… permanent service…'

Her father sank down onto his chair.

'You are hereby required… to join the Training Depot…'

What had happened to Dick, Norman, Stan, Arthur and Robert, was now happening to her father.

'At Winchester on Tuesday, 7th April…'

He'd come home with no arms or legs. Or if he had legs he wouldn't be able to walk on them.

'Should you not present yourself on that day you will be liable to be proceeded against.'

Or he'd be so badly burned she wouldn't recognise him.

'It's a mistake. It must be. Happens all the time...'

Her mother grabbed the letter.

'It's not you they want. It's another John Brown. There's enough of them...'

Her father buried his head in his hands.

'I registered as a volunteer, a year ago. Men with children, married men, I didn't think they'd...'

His mind so blown to bits all he would want to do is kill himself.

'I was wrong.'

If he ever came home at all.

FIVE

SAM SAT UP IN bed, her body knotted tight, her senses stretched thin. Her father was driving away from the home, where the three of them lived together, for what could be the last time. And she had overslept.

She hurled herself out of bed. She ran out of her room and along the landing towards the stairs. The door of her parents' bedroom opened.

'Sam?'

She kept running.

'Where are you going?'

She pulled open the front door, ran down the steps, down the path, through the gate and out onto the pavement. Her father's car was moving away, down the hill, towards the promenade. There was still time.

'Sam? What are you doing?'

She was grabbed from behind, so roughly that her arm was almost wrenched out of its socket.

'Come here.'

She twisted and turned but her mother's grip only tightened.

'Sam, enough of this, now, do you hear?'

The left indicator flashed. The car slowed down and then stopped. She dragged herself out of her mother's arms and ran, her feet slapping down hard against the wet tarmac. She didn't notice the sea, grey in the dawn, the first ferry of the day on its way over to France. She didn't see the streetlights, snaking away down the hill, switch off one by one. She just ran, the freezing cold rain beating up against the warmth of her body, towards the car where her father was sitting, leaning forward, clipping on his seat belt.

'Dad! Stop! Stop! Wait…'

But now the car was accelerating away. And still she pushed herself forward.

'Dad!' she screamed.

Seconds before, she'd been wearing jeans, jumper and socks, the clothes she'd gone to bed in, and she'd been shivering with cold. Now she was wearing a heavy coat, tightly laced boots and she was sweating. She had been running down the road towards her father's car. Now she was walking down a narrow footpath squeezed between a wire fence and high, brick wall. Who was she? Where was she going? What was she doing here? She had no option other than to obey the feet of the person whose clothes she was wearing.

A low, insistent drumming was getting, slowly and steadily, louder and nearer. A dull thump and the ground beneath her rocked and heaved. And now the drumming was no longer background, but foreground, drilling its way into every bone and sinew of her body. Up ahead, flying towards her out of the early morning sun, was a plane. Another thump was followed by another rock and heave. A huge ball of fire billowed up into the sky.

The footpath opened out into a yard between two derelict warehouses. The metallic throb of the plane's engine was so loud there might have been ten, twenty, thirty planes up there, flying towards her, rather than just the one.

Out here, if the plane dropped a bomb, she would be killed. She had to get inside. She ran towards the nearest warehouse. She pushed on the door. It stayed closed. She threw herself at the door. It refused to move. She tried one more time. Metal clanked down onto concrete. The door opened.

21

She was in a hallway. In front of her was a staircase lit by a single window. It would be safer on the ground floor. And she would be safer further inside. To her right was a set of double doors. She pushed. They opened easily. Ahead of her was the main storage area of the warehouse. It was empty and instead of being dark, which was what she had been expecting, it was light. She looked up. Above her was a glass roof. Directly over the roof was the plane.

A deep boom reverberated up towards the sky, the air around her shuddered, and then the warehouse disappeared in a blinding flash of white light.

The light faded to grey. And Sam was left, standing, trembling, in the middle of the road, staring at her father's car driving off into the distance.

'Sam, come on now, you're soaked through…'

How could she explain?

'I'll make us some tea.'

It had happened again, just like it had happened yesterday – the slip out of her life into another's.

'Why don't you run yourself a bath? Put on some dry clothes. I'll make us some breakfast…'

Sam pushed past her mother. She ran up the stairs, along the landing and into her bedroom. She grabbed her mobile. She punched in her father's number. If she rang enough times, again and again, there was a good chance that he would pull over and answer. But what was she going to say? That yesterday, at the fairground, she'd suddenly found herself standing on the platform of a station where hundreds of wounded were being loaded off a train? That she'd been running towards his car, the road had disappeared and then she was walking down a footpath and there was this plane flying towards her? She couldn't. He would think that she was crazy.

SIX

'BUT WHERE IS HE going to live?'

'I don't know Sam. He'll probably rent or share a flat or something...'

Her mother hurtled, without indicating, into the right hand lane of the roundabout.

'But will I still see him?'

'Of course you will.'

'But how? If he's always away and when he's at home, he's not living with us, but sharing a flat–'

'Everything will be all right.'

'But how will everything be all right?'

There were so many things that made her parents so different from each other that it was, perhaps, surprising they'd lasted together this long.

Her mother liked her garden to grow wild, so the plants, even the weeds, could reveal their true shape and character. Her father preferred to prune everything into order. Her mother's idea of heaven was a long, lazy afternoon sipping wine on the terrace of a Greek taverna. Her father didn't think a holiday was a holiday until he'd ridden the largest wave. Her mother disliked cars and anything to do with cars, describing them as 'boring, little metal boxes on wheels', while her father insisted on driving the largest and the fastest.

'We'll sort something out.'

'Like what?'

'Now what do you want for supper? I could do that new recipe…'

Her mother wasn't talking to Sam. She was talking at her as if she was a teacher standing on a platform at the front of the classroom and Sam was some rather small, stupid child, sitting down below, squeezed behind a desk.

'I saw it on the television, on that Saturday morning cookery programme…'

Sam closed her eyes. If she had a brother or sister, there would be someone to talk to, to share all this with.

'Rosemary chicken with tomato sauce…'

Her father had told her that when she was very small, not more than two years old, she'd had invisible friends. They'd come in the evening, after she'd been put to bed, when her mother was reading a story. These friends weren't children. When they walked into the room, she would look up, not down. And whoever, or whatever they were, she wasn't frightened of them. Her eyes would light up and she would laugh and giggle, tugging at her mother's hand, whenever they appeared.

But it gave her mother the spooks. When her father told her that she should be grateful that their daughter's invisible friends were at least people, not animals, lolloping, great horses galloping around the place, or heavy-weight tigers whose favourite past-time was lolling around on the sofa, her mother hadn't found it particularly funny.

She'd taken Sam straight to the doctor. He just laughed and said there wasn't anything to worry about. All children went through the invisible friends phase and, in Sam's case, it wasn't in the least surprising given she was an only child, but they ought to come back if the 'friends' were still around when she reached sixteen. Because then there really would be something to worry about.

And then one night, during a thunderstorm, her mother

had come into Sam's bedroom. She had expected to find her daughter curled up, shivering with fear, under the duvet. Instead she had found Sam standing on a stool, in front of the window, waving at the lightning forking through the sky. When, a few seconds later, thunder rumbled and cracked over the house Sam had jumped up and down, clapping her hands. How had she got onto the stool? It was too high even for the most determined two-year-old. And how had she opened the curtains? Which her father swore, again and again, he had pulled, tight shut, over the window before putting Sam to bed.

Her mother had insisted that they move; if Sam's invisible friends were ghosts, people who had died in the house, they would want to remain where they were, not follow them to their new home. Sam's father, a committed ghost non-believer, had agreed but very reluctantly.

So they left the two-hundred-year-old cottage, with its dark corners, low ceilings and sloping walls, in the town with a castle, a ruined priory and steep, cobbled streets. And they moved, just a half-hour drive away, to a newly built house, so new that it would be impossible for anyone to have had the time to die in it, on a hill overlooking the sea.

'Sam, did you hear what I said?'

There was a squeal of brakes followed by an angry honking. Sam opened her eyes. She was still alive. But only just.

'What would you like for supper? Because I'd like to have a go at that new recipe, rosemary chicken in tomato sauce? The one I was telling you about when you weren't listening?'

Her mother adored food; she talked about it endlessly, read every magazine, watched every television programme, browsed every website. But, after hours of slaving away in the kitchen whatever it was, a fish pie, spaghetti bolognese, even an omelette, would always end up a dried up, burnt disaster. Her father used to joke that if he hadn't learnt to throw a chop on a plate they would have starved. But the next time he flew back he would not be coming home.

'We could have baked potatoes. Or pasta...'

Her mother's phone rang out.

'Answer it, Sam.'

'Hello?'

There was a pause and then a voice asked if she was Mrs Rachel Foster.

'I'm Sam. Sam Foster. Rachel Foster's my mother.'

The voice asked if her mother was there and, if so, was it possible to speak to her.

'Mum, it's someone, a woman, she wants to speak to you.'

Her mother pulled up at the side of the road.

'It's probably the office...'

It was rare, very rare indeed, for her mother to get a phone call from work on a Sunday.

'Hello, Rachel Foster speaking.'

Sam stared out at the road ahead.

'Michael Foster? Yes, he's my husband.'

She darted a look across at her mother.

'He's been in an accident?'

The smile had been replaced by a tight-lipped frown.

'Which hospital?'

The knuckles of her mother's left hand, where she was grasping hold of the steering wheel, were white with tension.

'Yes. I understand. Thank you. I'll come straight away.'

SEVEN

April 1916

'ROCK-A-BYE BABY on the tree top...'

The official looking envelope, addressed to her father, with OHMS printed on the front, had been delivered just three days earlier.

'When the wind blows the cradle will rock...'

It had arrived on Saturday. Now it was Tuesday.

'When the bough breaks the cradle will fall...'

Her father had to report to the barracks in Winchester, a train journey away, no later than two o'clock.

'There's some cheese...'

Her mother's face was blotched and swollen with crying.

'And some pickle...'

Her father held her tight.

'... And down will come baby, cradle and all.'

It was the same lullaby her mother had sung to Jess when she was a baby. And now she was singing it to her brother.

Her father whispered something and then he pushed her mother gently back out of his embrace. He turned to Jess and lifted her brother out of her arms. He'd woken up, crying, in the middle of the night. He had continued to cry into the morning and was still crying now.

Her father bounced the kicking and screaming baby up and down, up and down, singing to him softly. Her brother's eyes fluttered, once, twice, and then closed – and stayed closed as her father handed him over to her mother.

'Jess, will you walk with me, just up the hill? Will you come with me?'

They were the same words she had said to her father, almost begged of him, the morning of her first day at school. And he had walked her, his large, strong hand holding her small, trembling hand, up the hill and down into the valley. But now, almost ten years later, as they walked down the path towards the gate, it was her hand that was steady and her father's that was trembling.

They climbed the white chalk track that led up onto the ridge. It was her favourite place, standing there on top of the world: to the east and west, Mount Caburn, Firle Beacon, Seaford Head, Kingston Hill and Hollingbury Castle; to the south, the English Channel stretching away to France; to the north, the fields and copses of the Weald rolling away, mile upon mile, towards London.

But now, standing there on top of the Downs, her father's smiling eyes had changed. They were like those of a fox, surrounded by a pack of hounds, knowing there was no escape.

She had seen the end of a chase, just the once, in the field at the bottom of Cradle Hill. She had been beside the stream, collecting firewood, when a fox had limped down towards her. It had sunk down, exhausted, in a ditch just a short distance from where she was standing.

'Come away now, Jess, there's nothing you can do.'

Her father had put his arm around her.

'The day we're born is the day we die. It don't matter if we're rich or poor, man, woman, or beast. When it's your time there's nothing you can do about it. We're all the same...'

Her father had led her away, along the path through the trees, as the hounds streamed down the slope to where the fox sat, hunched, waiting in the ditch.

The same father now stepped forward and put his arms around her. She buried herself in his familiar warmth.

'Promise me, however bad it gets… promise me, you'll not give up, not ever. Promise me…'

Usually, when she was standing up on the top of the Downs, it would be silent except for the wind sighing through the gorse bushes and the call of a solitary buzzard or kestrel circling overhead. But today there was a sound she'd never heard before; a low, insistent drumming which was getting, slowly and steadily, louder and nearer. Then, out of nowhere, without any warning, an enormous, white, insect-like object swooped down out of the sky.

She'd heard people talk about them. There had been pictures in the newspapers. But this was the first time she'd actually seen one.

'Look, a flying machine.'

She raised her arm to wave. Her father took hold of her wrist.

'Those black crosses on its wings, it's an enemy plane.'

'What's it doing here?'

His grip tightened.

'Go home now, Jess.'

'But –'

He pushed her away.

'Do as I say.'

She went back down the track. Every few paces she turned to look back. Each time her father was still there, exactly where she had left him. When she reached the bottom of the hill she turned and she waved. And he waved back.

She didn't move. She didn't turn off towards the cottage. She couldn't. She just stood there, waving and waiting. And when he gestured with his arm, she knew that he was saying, 'Go on, you must go home now'. And that is what she did, leaving him, a small, dark figure, standing alone on top of the hill, still waving.

EIGHT

March 1917

SHE LAY THERE, HUNCHED up beside her mother and her baby brother, underneath the mound of old clothes and blankets they had piled on top of the mattress to try and keep themselves warm.

The three of them shared the same bed. It had been four when her father had been at home; her parents in the middle, her baby brother between them, with Jess curled up on the edge of the lumpy, straw-filled mattress beside her mother. In the summer it was always too hot. Even with the window and the cottage door left open, she would lie there, tossing and turning, the flies buzzing around, desperately trying to get some sleep.

But it wasn't summer; it was the first week of March and the worst winter in living memory was continuing on into spring. There was still snow on the ground and more was expected. In the morning, the inside of the cottage's one window was coated with ice, which would melt during the day only to freeze up again when the sun went down. But this winter had been so cold that the ice never melted. It had stayed there, getting thicker by the day. There was no coal around, at least not in the village, and if there had been it would have been too expensive to buy. The only way to keep warm was to stay in bed.

But this morning, there was a glimmer of sunshine, the first Jess had seen for days, seeping through the threadbare blanket nailed up over the window.

She pulled on the boots that had been passed down to her by her mother four years ago. They were too large, had holes in the soles and had never had laces. Stuffed with balled up pages of newspaper, they stayed on unless she tried to run or kick something. She tugged a coat out of the pile of clothing heaped up on the bed. It had been repaired and patched so many times that there was almost nothing left of the original coat her mother had first worn, over twenty years ago, when she went up to London to go into service.

There was no sound, no movement, from the bed. Her mother must be still asleep. Jess walked across to the table. She opened the drawer and took out a knife, its blade tucked inside a leather sheath. She put it in the right hand pocket of the coat – the only pocket without a hole. She hesitated. A lump of stale bread, the size of her fist, was sitting on top of the table. Should she? Or shouldn't she? It was the only food they had left in the house. She slipped it into the same pocket.

A blast of cold air hit her as she stepped outside. With the sun out, and snow no longer falling, she wouldn't be the only one coming out to search for food. She slipped and slithered round the side of the cottage to the lean-to where her father kept his tools. She lifted the snare down off the hook, and the club down off the wooden shelf. She put both in a bag made out of sacking.

Down the garden, through the gate, and instead of turning left towards the lane, which led up onto the ridge, she turned right. Each morning her father had been away, and whatever the weather, sun, rain or snow, she'd followed this same path to the old oak that stood, alone and proud, in the centre of the field.

She drew her father's knife out of its sheath and scratched a line, the length of her little finger, deep down, into the bark of the old tree. One, two, three, four, five, six, seven. Seven lines. One more week. Today, it was exactly three hundred and eighteen days, just under eleven months, since her father had left for France.

In the summer, when the ground was dry, Butt's Brow was just a short walk away. But not today. There was either ice underfoot or mud, sometimes both. One foot slid to the right, the other to the left, leaving her struggling to stay upright. She tried cutting across the middle of a field but the mud was thicker, and even more slippery, than around the edge. One boot was sucked off then the other. She wanted to give up, turn around and go home, but she couldn't. Not without taking back some food.

The war that should have been over in four months was now into its third year. And the Germans, the enemy, weren't just fighting on land. They were also fighting at sea. The shelves in the grocer's shop were often empty: no sugar, no lard, no flour, as more and more merchant ships were torpedoed to the bottom of the ocean.

Her mother received an allowance of fourteen shillings a week from the government and her father sent home whatever he had managed to save out of his seven shillings a week wage. But the two combined came well below what he had been bringing home when he had worked as a labourer on the local farms. They lived off bread: a slice for breakfast, another slice for lunch and another slice in the afternoon for tea. And, if they were lucky, and her father had been able to send more money than usual, they had potatoes, plainly boiled, for supper. She couldn't remember the last time she'd eaten butter. But both the bread and the potatoes had doubled in price. A single loaf now cost one whole, precious silver shilling.

Summer, late afternoon, was the best time to catch a rabbit. Today, on this icy cold morning, she would be lucky to get one. But this was where her father always came. And rabbits, like humans, had to eat. Jess set the snare and then placed the bait – the lump of stale bread. She crouched down behind a bush.

Just as the sun was dipping below the trees, a young doe hopped out of a burrow. It sniffed, sniffed again and took another hop forward. It took a nibble at the bread. Its head went through the noose. Another nibble, another hop and it was trapped, the wire round its neck getting tighter and tighter with every frantic kick and wriggle. Jess raised her father's club. The rabbit thrashed from side to side. The snare snapped. And the pie, soup and dumplings, that would have kept the three of them fed for a whole week, hopped down into a burrow.

Her mother said nothing when Jess showed her the broken snare. When she tried to explain about the lump of bread, how it too had disappeared, with the rabbit, down into the burrow, her mother just turned away. There would be nothing to eat that night. Not for anyone.

NINE

April 1917

SHE WAS CROUCHED DOWN in the gutter, in the centre of the cobbled street, and she was about to do what her father and mother had always forbidden her to do. But she had no choice.

On each of the three hundred and twenty-eight days that her father had been away, Jess had listened to the clink and clatter of metal on wood, as her mother separated the precious silver shillings, and then the bronze pennies, half pennies and farthings into four neat piles on top of the table. And when her mother had counted each individual coin, in each separate pile, Jess had counted too, in a whisper, so that she could not be heard.

Over the weeks and the months, the piles of coins had gone down from four to three as the shillings had disappeared, then the pennies and then the half pennies. Last night, when her mother had picked up the blue and white jug, there had been no clinking and no whispering; there had been no coins to count, none at all, not even a single brass farthing.

Jess crawled, on her knees, round and through a queue of people, under a market stall and up to a shopping basket. She stretched out a hand. The bread was still warm. And with the warmth came anger. Anger that a stranger could afford to buy this bread while she, her mother and her brother were being forced to live off nettles, dandelions, and turnip tops.

The loaf was large, too large to hide. She ripped off one end and, crouching forward, knotted it inside the frayed cotton of her underskirt. She put the rest of the loaf back in the basket with the torn end facing down. She crawled out from under the stall. She staggered to her feet and, with the stolen bread bouncing awkwardly against her legs, walked as fast as she could, so fast she was almost running, across the road to the opposite side of the street. Pushing through a line of women queuing up to buy food, she was about to step into the safety of an alleyway when she stopped to look back.

A woman was staring at her. She was wearing a tightly buttoned grey coat and on her right arm there was a black mourning band. At her feet, on the ground, was the shopping basket and inside it, torn side up, was the loaf of bread.

Jess wanted to run, slip away into the darkness, but her body, her legs, refused to obey. And then the woman nodded her head, so slight but still a nod, and the force that had prevented Jess from moving released its hold.

She ducked into the alley. Walls towered up on either side. Turning left and then right, then left and right again, she came out at the bottom of the main street just in front of the flint-stone church.

She took the right fork, running on past the post boy pushing his bicycle, inch by inch, up the hill. Houses gave way to cottages, the cottages to fields. The road narrowed into a white chalk track. She looked ahead and behind. No one was following her. She unknotted the bread from inside her underskirt. She sniffed it. She nibbled a corner. It was her due; she'd had the idea, she'd taken the risk and she'd done the running. Her mother would never know. She sank her teeth down into its doughy warmth.

She was standing exactly where she and her father had stood almost a year ago, the morning he had left home to go to the barracks at Winchester. Down below, on the other side of the ridge, she could see their cottage, tucked away at the edge of the woods, at the bottom of the valley.

The door was shut and the curtains drawn. There was no smoke curling out of the chimney and there was no washing hanging out on the line. And the garden, where her mother had spent so much of her time, digging up, clearing and planting vegetables, was now choked with weeds. The cottage was no longer a home: it was a tomb.

She ran down the track, through the gate and up the path to the door. She tore down the blanket she had helped her mother to nail up at the start of the winter. It was time to let in some fresh air and sunshine.

'Mum, Mum, I've got us some bread.'

The figure curled up on the bed, under the mound of clothes and blankets, shifted.

'Look, Mum, bread, I've got us some bread.'

Her mother sat up.

'We can't afford bread...'

Her mother took hold of her arm.

'How did you get it? Did you steal it?'

Her grip tightened.

'Did you? Tell me, did you steal it?'

'It was a present, a present from a lady in the market...'

'What have you been doing? Why would a lady like that want to give people like us a present?'

'She felt sorry for us.'

She felt no guilt, none whatsoever, sitting at the kitchen table, watching her mother feeding pieces of bread, soaked in water, to her baby brother. It didn't matter that the bread had been stolen. She was keeping them alive, making sure they would all still be there to welcome her father when he came back home.

She could see it. A summer's evening, the sun dropping down behind the trees, her mother, holding her brother, both plump cheeked and laughing, and herself, standing in the doorway, watching her father dressed in his soldier's

36

uniform, a pack on his back, stride down the hill towards the cottage.

There was a loud rap. Her mother looked up.

'See who that is, Jess.'

She knew who it was. She didn't have to open the door. It was her father. He was standing there, smiling, waiting to be let in, his head cocked to one side, his fingers tapping impatiently.

'Jess? Did you hear?'

He would get his old job back on the farm. They would be able to afford medicine for her brother and coal for the fire to keep them warm. There would be stews bubbling on the range and mugs of steaming hot tea and slabs of fresh bread, with butter and a slice of cheese, sometimes even ham, for a treat on a Sunday. They would be happy. They would be a family again.

She opened the door.

'Mrs. Brown? Edith Brown?'

The post boy wiped the sweat off his face with the back of his hand.

'That's my mother.'

Jess took the brown envelope with OHMS printed on the front.

'Thank you.'

The post boy walked away down the path.

She closed the door. She tore open the envelope. She took out the sheet of paper. She unfolded the letter.

"It is my duty to inform you that a report has been received from the War Office notifying the death of William John Brown."

TEN

'YOU DID SAY MR. Foster?'

The receptionist checked her computer.

'Mr. Michael Foster.'

It had taken half an hour to get there. One minute her mother was upset. The next minute she was angry. At every left turn, right turn, traffic light, roundabout and T-junction, she repeated that Sam's father was fine. He was at the airport. The hospital had phoned the wrong person.

'Yes. That's right. Look, there's been some mistake. My husband—'

'Seaview Road. Number seven? That's the address he's given us. Is that where you live, Mrs Foster?

'Yes...'

It was her father. So how had the accident happened? It was impossible to believe that he had caused it; he was too careful a driver. Unlike her mother who thought nothing of overtaking in the inside lane and always accelerated when the traffic lights were changing to red, her father obeyed every chapter, paragraph, sentence, comma and full stop of the Highway Code.

If it said check your mirror, he checked it not twice but three times. Too much to the left, too much to the right, too much sticking out the front, too much sticking out the back, parking a car was no different to docking a Boeing; it required exactly the same amount of precision. All that was missing was the man wearing the metal earmuffs, walking backwards, waving him in.

'Mrs Foster, if you'd just like to take a seat, I'll let them know you're here.'

Her mother's mobile shrilled out.

'It's Dad's work. Hello, yes, Rachel Foster speaking...'

Her father never drank the day before he flew. Whether they were having supper out or giving a party, it was a rule he would never break, not ever, however great the temptation. And last night would have been no different.

'Yes, we're at the hospital. We've only just got here. Yes, in the accident and emergency department. No, Mike didn't phone. The hospital did. Yes, I will, as soon as I know. No problem. Bye.'

'Mrs Foster?'

'Yes?'

'Hi, I'm Kelly, one of the team looking after your husband. If you'd like to follow me...'

Sam had expected crowds of disgruntled people, some drunk, many of them shouting. But the waiting area was empty except for a smartly dressed couple, sitting together, holding hands, talking quietly to themselves, and a young man in a hoodie eyeing up the refreshment machine. Nobody was bleeding.

Her mother had fallen over, several years ago, when carrying a large blue and white bowl from the sitting room into the kitchen. A piece of broken china had embedded itself into her leg, just below the knee. She'd insisted on pulling it out there and then. Blood had sprayed everywhere, all over her mother, all over the floor, all down the cupboards. The next thing Sam remembered was hearing someone repeating her name. When she opened her eyes she was lying on the kitchen floor and her mother, sitting upright on a chair with a blood-soaked towel knotted round her knee, was asking her father whether he thought they should take Sam to a hospital.

'Your husband was brought in by ambulance, Mrs Foster.'

'But how did it happen? My husband's a pilot. He flies planes...'

They walked through a set of double doors. Stretching out in front of them was another white-walled corridor.

'Yes, he's told us.'

Kelly's smile was tight-lipped.

'He also told us that he was on his way to work, driving along, and there was a girl standing on the pavement. She walked out right in front of him. Whether it was accidental, she didn't see him coming, or deliberate we don't know. Your husband's given the police a description.'

'Has he been badly hurt, the person who phoned didn't say?'

'His seatbelt was faulty. When he braked, to avoid hitting her, he went straight into the windscreen. Got quite a nasty knock on the head...'

They stopped. The corridor widened out. There was a line of cubicles on either side. Each individual cubicle contained a couple of chairs and a lamp attached to the wall over a trolley bed. But only one had a curtain drawn across its entrance.

'The x-rays and scan show nothing abnormal but your husband really should stay here overnight, for observation, to make sure that everything is fine, just in case there is any complication, but he won't hear of it. We were rather hoping you might be able to get him to change his–'

Her mother shook her head.

'You've got the wrong person...'

The cubicle curtain jerked open. And there was her father.

'I want my car keys, I want my mobile, and I want them now.'

'He only listens to his auto-pilot.'

The doors they had just walked through crashed open. A trolley, surrounded by doctors and nurses, smashed past. Lying on the trolley was an elderly man. As the trolley crashed through a second set of double doors at the far end of the corridor, Sam caught a glimpse of a brilliantly lit, white room with figures, wearing gloves, face masks and green overalls, standing round what looked like an operating table.

ELEVEN

'Yes, on the corner of Stanley Road and Mortimer Street. Yes, the keys are in the usual place. Yes, that's right. No problem. Tomorrow will be fine. Cheers.'

Her father clicked off his phone.

'They'll collect the car today, fix the seatbelt and then bring it back over here, to the house, tomorrow, probably in the morning.'

Everything was going to be all right.

'Your head looks awful. Does it hurt?'

They were almost home.

'Bit of a bruise. That's all.'

And her mother and father were talking to each other.

'Are you sure they said no flying for two weeks?'

'At least two weeks. You were there when they said it…'

Her mother swerved right into a side street. A car travelling towards them, down the main road, slammed on its brakes.

'Rachel…'

Her mother slowed.

'You didn't even indicate…'

The car stopped.

'You don't just–'

Sam slid down into her seat. She closed her eyes.

'Get out.'

Her father laughed.

'Rachel…'

He was sitting in his cockpit.

'I said get out.'

Her mother was standing on her platform.

'Because if you don't like the way I drive then do me a favour and get out of my car.'

They sat there, in silence, the three of them going nowhere, her mother tapping her fingers against the steering wheel.

'I'm sorry.'

The tapping stopped.

'Apology accepted.'

The car moved forward. Sam opened her eyes. This time her mother indicated.

'So will you be OK, the two of you, if I go and get the shopping? Because we could send out for a delivery this evening...'

Her mother was holding her car keys but there was no sign of her moving out of the kitchen, along the hall, out of the front door and into her car. She was stuck.

'We could have a pizza or we could try out the new Indian place in Portland Street. They both do home–'

'I'll go and get the shopping.'

Her father grabbed the keys out of her hand.

'You can't.'

He was at the door.

'You mustn't drive. I was there when they told you.'

Her mother snatched the keys back from him.

'Not for at least three days.'

The front door slammed. Her father sank down onto a chair. He sat there, silent, head in his hands, slumped down over the table.

'Dad, everything's going to be all right, isn't it?'

Her father lifted his head.

'Please, Sam...'

'With you and Mum...'

Her father closed his eyes. He shook his head, slowly, from side to side.

'Not now, please.'

'You won't have to leave, will you?'

He stood up.

'I'm going upstairs to change. Get out of this uniform…'

He walked out of the kitchen, slamming the door shut behind him.

She would make his favourite sandwich: cheddar cheese and oak-smoked ham on granary with honey mustard. She would take it upstairs and he would laugh and give her a hug. Her mother would come back from the supermarket. They would unpack the shopping and there would be chicken casserole in tomato sauce, with anchovies, garlic and capers, for supper.

She sliced and buttered the bread. She added a slice of cheese, some mustard, another slice of ham, some more mustard and then another slice of cheese. Her father liked his sandwiches big, very big. But he also liked them very neat and very orderly.

There was a thump of feet down the stairs and along the hallway. The door opened and her father stumbled into the kitchen – or rather the ghost of her father. In less than ten minutes, in the time it had taken for her to prepare the sandwich, he had turned into a stooped and frail old man.

'Sam…'

He clutched at her hand.

'Please…'

'Dad? What's happened? What's the matter?'

His mouth twisted, contorted, but no words came, only a trail of spittle.

'Dad…'

He sank down onto the kitchen floor and, twisting himself up tight into a ball, began to whimper.

'Si…'

His body juddered and juddered again, uncontrollably. He started to retch.

She jumped up and grabbed the plastic washing up bowl from the cupboard underneath the sink. She crouched back down beside her father.

'Dad?'

It was stupid but she held out the bowl. Her father pushed it away. He slid down to one side, his head and upper body propped up against a kitchen cupboard. He coughed, then retched and coughed again. His mouth opened and he vomited, helplessly, all over everything and everywhere, including himself.

She scrambled, gagging from the smell, up on to her feet. She snatched up her mobile and punched in her mother's number. It rang. And rang. And rang. There was silence, followed by a click, and then her mother's laughing voice told her to leave a message.

'Mum. It's me, Sam. It's Dad, he's really ill, he's been sick and everything. I don't know what to do, come home, please, come home...'

Her father was still lying there, slumped down against the cupboard, but his eyes were now closed. Her mother had left twenty minutes ago. It was a ten-minute drive to the supermarket. She wouldn't be back for at least half an hour.

Sam punched in the three digit number she had always assumed, in her previous life, the one she had been living just fifteen minutes ago, she would never have to dial.

'Ambulance, please. Yes. Number seven, Seaview Road. Yes. Seaview Road. That's right. It's my father. My name? My name is Sam, Sam Foster.'

How long would the ambulance take to get there? Ten minutes? Fifteen? She put the phone down. She was trembling, not just her hand, but her whole body.

TWELVE

THE TROLLEY CRASHED THROUGH the double doors into a brilliantly lit, white room. Figures, wearing gloves, face masks and green overalls, stood round what looked like an operating table.

'Sam? It is Sam, isn't it? You came in this morning. With your mother…'

An arm was placed around her shoulder and she was led away, down a corridor, round a corner and into a room. The nurse called Kelly asked if she would like something to drink, a tea or a coffee. Sam replied. A door closed. And there was silence.

She sat there, her body clenched tight, her eyes unseeing, her mind blank, conscious of each and every beat of her heart, each short, sharp gasp for air. If she allowed herself just for a second to let go, everything, her mind, body, the room in which she was sitting, would spiral out of control.

A door opened. A cup and saucer was put down on the table in front of her. Kelly asked if she was all right and then said that her mother was on her way to the hospital. The door closed. Silence.

She lifted her head and looked around. The walls of the room were white. To her right, where she would have expected to see a window, there was a blank wall. She looked down. The carpet under her feet was a dull grey and she was sitting on a dull grey sofa. There were two armchairs, the same dull grey, one on either side of the sofa. Hanging on the wall to the left of the door, was a picture of a blue vase containing pink flowers. The flowers were roses and the vase was standing on a shelf in front of an open window. Beyond the window was a sun-filled garden.

Directly in front of her was a low table. On the table was a large box of paper tissues and the cup and saucer. She picked up the cup and took a sip. It was coffee and it was cold. What had seemed like seconds had, in fact, been minutes.

Voices and footsteps, the tip, tap of heels, getting nearer. Her body tensed. The door opened.

'I got your message and went straight home and you weren't there.'

It was her mother.

'Then my mobile rang and it was the hospital and–'

'Would you like something to drink, Mrs Foster?'

'Coffee would be lovely, thank you,' said her mother.

The nurse, called Kelly, turned to go. Sam wanted to go with her, to run away from this room without a view, but the door closed and she and her mother were left alone.

'What happened? When I went out Dad was fine…'

Sam didn't know what to do: whether she should sit, whether she should stand, say something or stay silent. Everything she did, or didn't do, would be wrong.

'And he was talking and walking, not being sick, and he didn't have a headache…'

Sam searched for words but with the words came pictures, and neither the words nor the pictures contained a single scrap of comfort. She was back crouched down beside her father, where he lay, barely breathing and unconscious, on the kitchen floor. She could hear the tick, tock, tick, tock of the clock, getting louder and louder, hammering its way inside her head. And she was praying and she was crying for the ambulance to come.

'Hello. I'm Dr. Brownlow.'

He looked no older than some of the boys at her school. But he was smiling.

'Please do sit down, Mrs Foster.'

Her mother took a half step towards the other empty chair, hesitated and then sank down next to Sam on the sofa.

'Mrs Foster, we suspect that your husband has had a subdural haematoma, a form of intracranial mass lesion. It's likely to be acute rather than sub acute, or chronic, but until we do a scan we won't know for certain. The scan will take place, here, at the hospital, as a matter of urgency, as soon as your husband's been stabilised.'

He paused to re-load.

'Your husband has been transferred to the intensive care unit on the top floor. You'll be able to go up to see him soon…'

'But how, why, did this happen? Was it because of this morning, the car accident, the knock he received on his head?'

'Mrs Foster, the answer to your question is almost certainly yes, but we won't be able to confirm that until we've had the results of the scan. We would have liked to have kept your husband in, under observation, just in case, but as you know he refused…'

There was a tap on the door. The doctor jumped to his feet.

'Kelly, here, will look after you.'

The door closed, and he was gone.

'Two coffees?'

Kelly placed the two cups and saucers down on the table. The door opened. The door closed. And, once again, Sam and her mother were alone, sitting side by side on the dull grey sofa, both staring, fixedly, at cups of dull grey coffee.

'If I'd known I would never have gone out. Maybe if I'd been there…'

Her mother being there, at home, wouldn't have stopped

any of this happening. The 'just in case', which everyone had been so worried about, had happened. Sam stood up.

'Sam, are you all right? Where are you going?'

'I need the toilet.'

It was a lie but she had to get out of that room.

'"I have some bad news and some very bad news."'

Two men, one tall, one short, were sauntering down the corridor towards her. The tall one had long hair. The short one had none. Both were wearing identical security guard uniforms. It was the tall one who was doing the talking.

'And the patient said, "Well, you might as well give me the bad news first." And the doctor said, "The lab called with your test results. They said you have twenty-four hours to live."'

The short man snorted. The tall man continued.

'"Twenty-four hours! That's terrible! What could be worse? What's the very bad news?" The doctor said, "I've been trying to reach you since yesterday."'

A door down the corridor, to her right, had a 'Ladies' sign on it. Only one of the three cubicles was occupied. Sam turned on the tap. She leant over and splashed cold water onto her face. There was a rustle from inside the cubicle and then a click. The door opened. A girl dressed in black walked out of the cubicle. She was crying. Sam turned round.

'Are you...'

There was a flash of red, blue and silver, and the girl was gone.

THIRTEEN

May 1917

GAUNT-FACED, SUNKEN-EYED women and children stared out of cottage doorways as the horse and cart creaked down the hill towards the church. Her mother sat in the front, dressed in the frayed black mourning dress that had been passed down through the family, from mother to daughter, for as long as anyone could remember. And now it was her mother's turn to wear it.

She had put on the dress the morning after the post boy had delivered the letter telling them that Jess' father had been killed in action. On her lap she cradled a tiny white coffin. A funeral was nothing new. So many children had died and so many children, young and not so young, some the same age as Jess, had been buried. Her brother was just one more.

He had taken over a month to die. Day after day, night after night, he lay there in the bed, disappearing into himself. His breath, at first loud and harsh, gradually became quieter and softer. Then one day, when she woke up, she was aware that the shrunken little body lying in the bed beside her was no longer warm. It was cold, stone cold. Her brother had passed away in the night when she and her mother were sleeping. The cause of his death was starvation. That was two days ago.

A man, his body bent and twisted from polio, bowed his head as the horse and cart creaked past his cottage. Two children, one girl, one boy, stood on either side of him. His wife, their mother, had died in childbirth the year before. After her death, he'd sent his son and daughter to the local children's home thinking, now they had no mother, it would be the best place for them to go; they would be better looked after there than at home. Jess remembered the hugs and kisses, the tearful goodbyes, at the end of their last day at school.

A month later and Harry and Clare were back. They'd run away from the home. But the two children who walked into the playground were very different from the two children who had walked out. They'd always been stick thin, and that hadn't changed, but now their bodies, including their faces, were covered in sores and bruises.

Hunched down at the far end of the playground, Clare and Harry sitting in the centre of the circle, Jess and the rest of the class had listened, wide-eyed, as the brother and sister described how they'd had to scrub floors, mop steps and prepare the food (oatmeal boiled up in lukewarm water with the occasional bit of bone or lump of turnip). They weren't allowed to talk, run or laugh. They were beaten for not sleeping with their legs straight and beaten again for demanding to be called by their own names, Harry and Clare, rather than just numbers sixty-two and sixty-three. Their father let them stay at home. To die of starvation, loved, was better than dying of starvation, unloved.

The first drops of rain fell as the horse and cart drew to a halt outside the church's lychgate. It had seen many a wedding and christening. Now it was seeing the funerals. The driver didn't move, just sat there wrapped up in his greatcoat, slapping the reins impatiently against the quivering flanks of his scrawny horse. Anything reasonably fit, whether horse, mule or pony, had long ago been loaded onto a ship and sent across the Channel to serve with the army in France. The few that remained to plough the fields, pull the carts, or heave coal down the pits were either too old, too sick or too small.

Jess jumped down, drawing her shawl up over her head, and ran round, feet splashing through puddles, to where her mother was sitting. Her mother slid the coffin towards her. For something so small it seemed surprisingly heavy, far heavier than when they first left the cottage half an hour ago. She supported the coffin against her stomach, leaning it up against the side of the cart, while her mother clambered down. Together, one at either end, they carried it through the lychgate and across the churchyard to where a single, black-robed figure stood, umbrella up and bible in hand, by a newly dug grave.

"'I am the resurrection and the life," saith the Lord. "He that believeth in me, though he were dead, yet shall he live…"'

The men and boys from the village, the ones who had been so loudly clapped and cheered as they marched off to war, would never be laid to rest in this churchyard. Her father was buried somewhere in France, possibly in a military cemetery or just in a hole dug in the side of a trench. They didn't know, and might never know, where.

"'And whosoever liveth and believeth in me shall never die…"'

At least with her brother they had something to say goodbye to. Her mother had insisted on doing it properly however much it cost. She now received a widow's pension, and had used up most of that month's allowance, even smaller than the one she'd had before, to buy the coffin, the grave and the hasty words of prayer that were now being said over it.

'We therefore commit his body to the ground; earth to earth, ashes to ashes, dust to dust in the sure and certain hope of the Resurrection to eternal life.'

Rain ripped through the graveyard sending the vicar, his black gown billowing out behind him, running back to the shelter of his church.

They stood there, mother and daughter, shivering with cold, their threadbare clothes soaked through, the wind and rain gusting and swirling around them, staring down at the mud-splattered white coffin. Her mother pulled a posy of primroses out of her pocket. She threw the flowers down into the waterlogged grave.

A woman dressed in a tightly buttoned grey coat, a black mourning band on her right arm, was kneeling beside a grave on the opposite side of the churchyard. The woman stood. She brushed clods of mud off her coat, picked up her basket and walked, between the rows of gravestones, over to where Jess and her mother were standing.

It was the woman from the market, the one she'd stolen the bread from, would she say something? The woman glanced down at the coffin and then looked up. She stared at Jess, hesitated and then turned to her mother.

'I'm sorry for your loss.'

Her mother nodded.

'And we for yours.'

The woman bowed her head and walked on, past Jess and her mother, down the path and out through the lychgate.

FOURTEEN

'COME ON, JESS, LOOK sharp. He'll be here soon.'

She slipped out from under the blankets. The bed, which had been originally shared by four, then three, was now only slept in by two. Soon it would be just one.

She took a sip of tea. The primroses had long gone, the bluebells were fading and the elderflowers were almost out. Summer was just a few weeks away but inside the cottage, tucked away in the valley at the bottom of the hill, the mornings were still bitterly cold.

'These tea leaves are the ones I used the morning your father left...'

The last breakfast the family had eaten, sitting together round the table, her mother bouncing the screaming baby up and down on her lap.

'I dried them, saved them up for the day he was coming home...'

Her mother stood up.

'And now you're going...'

London wasn't that far away.

'I'll come and visit whenever I can. They'll let me do that, won't they?'

Her mother poured water from the jug into the chipped enamel basin.

'I won't have you going up there dirty...'

She picked up a cloth.

'Come on, stand over here, where I can get at you...'

Jess walked round the table to her mother.

'Up they go.'

Jess raised her arms. With no money, coal too expensive to buy, and with only a few twigs left for firewood, having a bath, even one every two or three months, was no longer possible. A quick scrub with a piece of cloth had to do. But in the winter it had been too cold to do even that. Her mother had sewn Jess into her winter clothes in November and, she'd stayed in them, day and night, never taking them off – until now.

'I met your father at the house. He delivered the vegetables, in his barrow, fresh from the market at Covent Garden. We ate a lot of vegetables, all those people in a big, grand house like that…'

Jess winced. She wouldn't have any body left if her mother kept scrubbing so hard.

'There would be potatoes and onions and leeks for us servants, and asparagus and beans and peas, for the family, the Major, his wife and the boys. Boxes and boxes we had delivered. Didn't know where to put them there were so many. The artichokes were the worst. Nasty prickly things, all leaves and stalk and worms…'

Her mother rinsed out the cloth.

'And in the summer we had lettuce, all sorts, floppy ones, crinkly ones, and radishes and tomatoes and cucumber. The Major was a meat man but if his vegetables were wrapped up in pastry or hidden away under a sauce where he couldn't see them, a white one with nutmeg, sometimes cook would add cheese, or onions, cooked long and slow, then he would eat them.'

The water in the basin was now black with over six months' dirt. Her mother held out the cloth.

'You finish yourself off, properly now, while I get your things ready.'

Jess lifted her shift and scrubbed.

'You might meet your own husband there.'

Her mother knelt down beside the shiny, new leather suitcase sitting on the floor. She lifted the lid.

'Like I did.'

What chance did she, Jess, have of finding a boyfriend, let alone a husband? There were no young men. There were none left. They were all out in France fighting the war. Or dead.

'Come on, take off that shift…'

Jess hesitated. When she'd been a little girl she'd never been embarrassed about running around, in front of her mother and father, as naked as the day she was born. But her body had changed.

'You'd best be quick…'

She pulled off her stained and torn shift and took the one her mother was holding out. She'd never seen anything so white.

'You're a fine girl, Jess.'

Her mother looked her up and down and smiled.

'Some might even say pretty…'

Jess pulled on the shift.

'It's scratchy…'

'A couple of washes will soften it up.'

On went the woollen dress, the black stockings and the ankle boots, all bought with the money sent down from London.

'Wrap the bottom lace over and through the top lace…'

She watched, and tried to remember, as her mother looped, knotted and tied a bow.

Lastly, she pulled on, and buttoned, the black wool coat.

'It's so big…'

The sleeves reached down over her fingers. The bottom almost touched the floor.

'You'll grow into it. That's what happened, when I went up to London, to a big house, with decent food to eat.'

Her mother picked up the suitcase.

'Get off the train and don't move, just stay there. The Major's a big man, big all over. And he always swings his arms like he's marching. And no hair, even when he was young...'

And there was the cart drawn by the horse, its head sagging, eyes rolling, ribs sticking out, crawling along the mud-choked track towards them. It was the same cart and the same horse, with the same driver wrapped up warm inside his coat, which had taken them to the church for her brother's funeral less than three weeks ago.

His death was a blessing. He had gone to heaven. It was the end of his suffering. This was what her mother had repeated, again and again, as they trudged, slipping and sliding in the mud, out of the village, up the hill and then down the hill back to the cottage.

There was no heaven. At least not like the one preached about in the church on Sunday. How could there be angels with haloes and wings? How could Jesus rise from the dead? How could anyone rise from the dead? It was all impossible. How could you believe in a God, or anything like a God, with the war out in France, and all the men and boys dying, and all the women and children sick and starving?

The one thing she could understand, really understand, was the need to feel no further pain. To be dead, to be nothing, to disappear into a hole in the ground, had to be better than spitting, coughing and vomiting your life away as her brother had done the last weeks, days and hours of his life. She knew what that was. She didn't need the bible or a preacher to tell her. That was hell.

But this cart with its near-dead horse was taking her away to a new and better life.

'Now be a good girl, Jess.'

Her mother hugged her tight.

'Work hard and do what you're told and you'll be well looked after.'

Jess slid her suitcase onto the cart and then climbed up after it. The driver flicked his reins. The cart shuddered forward. Jess turned to look back. And there was her mother, a small, dark figure, standing alone at the bottom of the hill, still waving.

FIFTEEN

THEY WERE IN THE intensive care unit and she was walking, head down, eyes fixed on the scuffed heels of her mother's brown leather boots, because she was scared of what she was going to see when eventually they stopped – and she would have to raise her head and look. They passed one bed, two beds, three beds; there was a scrape, a shuffle, a murmur of voices and then her mother's feet disappeared underneath a chair.

Sam raised her head and stared. She kept on staring in the hope, that if she stared long enough and hard enough, her eyes would swallow up the nightmare; the man, his body punctured with tubes, lying on the bed. She looked more closely. She searched for detail but the more she looked, the more she saw, the pallid skin, the sweat-soaked hair, the blue veins on the back of the hand, the less she could believe, and the less she wanted to believe, that this thing, that was barely human, that looked like a robot out of a sci-fi film, was her father.

Sam glanced over to where her mother was sitting, back straight, eyes wide, her hands clamped onto her handbag as though her life, their lives, the whole world as they knew it, depended on the continued existence of the handbag and everything in it.

Sam recognised that need. It was exactly the same need that had made her get up off the floor, walk over to the sink, pick up the plastic bowl and then go back down to kneel beside her father, holding out the bowl towards him, so that, please, if he was going to be sick, then could he do so, not all over himself, the cupboards and the floor, but into the plastic bowl – so that everything could be kept nice and neat and clean and tidy.

But nothing was nice and neat and clean and tidy. Her father, the same father who hadn't hesitated to risk his own life in order to save hers, was now lying, hooked up to machines, in the intensive care unit of the local hospital.

Years ago, when she was old enough to have a memory, but not old enough to put that memory into any context, they had gone, the three of them, herself, her mother and her father, out for the day to a village where some distant, long dead, relative used to live. At that age she had very little understanding of how short or long a minute, an hour, even a day, was. A month was completely incomprehensible, a year even more so. Time was measured by how happy, unhappy or, even, how bored she was. An unhappy minute could seem longer than a day, a happy hour shorter than a minute. But Sam knew she was quite happy, even very happy, as happy as she'd ever been, sitting there, looking out of the window, the sunlight flooding in, listening to music while her parents laughed and chatted away to each other in the front of the car.

They got to where they were supposed to be going. They visited a church, stared at a gravestone and then had something to eat. Whether it was lunch or tea she couldn't remember. The next memory she had was walking between her mother and father along a path, then up a steep flight of steps onto a narrow, wooden bridge. A whistle and a hoot echoed up the valley. They stopped to wave as an old steam train rattled past on the other side of the river.

To the right, the river flowed slow and smooth while, to her left, it tumbled down a weir. And then, for some reason, instantly, there and then, she was filled with a desperation that could not be explained. She tugged, hard, even violently, she might even have kicked out, her father let go of her hand and she plunged down, off the bridge and into the river.

She was under the water, and then she was on top of it. And then she was under it again. She surfaced, gulping for air. People were running up and down the riverbank. A motorboat, a white one, was speeding towards her. The last thing she saw, as the river closed over her head, was her father diving off the bridge into the water.

Her next memory was opening her eyes to find herself lying on the ground with a crowd of people looking down at her. There were nods and smiles. Someone asked if they should call an ambulance. Her father said no, everything was fine, thank you. And then the people wandered off – and her mother started. And she went on and on, all the way to the car and all the way home. Sam could have drowned. Her father had to dive in to save her. He could have been killed.

That evening, back at home, her father came up to her room. He sat down on the bed beside her.

'Sam, you mustn't be upset. Mummy only said the things she said because she loves you and she's terrified of losing you.'

He squeezed her hand.

'Those invisible friends, the ones you used to see in your bedroom in our old house…'

What they looked like, their names, she had no memory of them, nothing at all.

'If they do come back, if you see them again, you will tell us, won't you?'

What she could remember was waking up in a bedroom she didn't recognise, in a house she didn't know, and being told that this was her new home.

'Will we have to move again?'

Her father laughed.

'I hope not.'

He stood up.

'You mustn't worry. But what happened today, on the bridge, was a bit strange…'

She didn't then, all those years ago, translate into words the feeling of desperation that had flooded through her while she was walking across that bridge on that sunny Saturday afternoon. Everything had been so perfect, so peaceful, and then suddenly, without any warning, out of nowhere, all that had mattered, her mother's laughter, the touch of her father's hand, the warmth of the sun on her face, all of it became meaningless.

Yesterday, the three of them had been a happy family. And now the same thing had happened. Joy and pleasure had, in a blink of an eye, been replaced by misery and despair.

'It would be best if you went home now. Have something to eat, get some rest.'

The young doctor who had talked to the two of them so briskly in the accident and emergency department was standing, sleeves rolled up, stethoscope still draped round his neck, at the head of her father's bed.

'Tomorrow at ten we'll go through the results of the scan. We'll ring if there's any change.'

SIXTEEN

HER MOTHER REMAINED SILENT, not speaking a single word, eyes fixed on the road ahead, all the way back from the hospital.

When they passed the angel statue and turned left, off the promenade, to drive up the hill, the house was still there, standing in a row, with all the other houses. It was identical to the one she had left earlier that afternoon with her father in the ambulance.

It was the same height, and the same width, it had the same number of windows, the same front garden, and the same path leading up to the same front door. But at the same time it looked and felt completely different – it was a stranger to her. Another family lived there, another mother and father with a spiky blonde-haired daughter called Sam, not her own.

The curtains, which her mother had sewn together out of material she'd picked up at a car boot sale, were still hanging downstairs in the front window. In the summer, when all Sam wanted to do was spend every minute of every day down on the beach, the multi-coloured stripes fluttering cheerfully in the sunshine had encouraged her, waved her on, as she trudged up the hill after a very long and very boring day cooped up at school. Drooping there in the window, the same curtains now looked dreary, even desperate.

Her mother parked the car in the usual place. Still in silence, her mother ahead, Sam trailing along behind, they walked up the garden path towards the front door. Her mother put her key in the lock. Sam expected it to jam, the door to be opened by a woman who would look at them in puzzlement before telling them that they must have come to the wrong house.

The key turned and the door got stuck where it always got stuck. Her mother kicked and it opened. They walked into the hallway. There were the boots piled up in the basket to the right of the front door and the same coats, her dark blue one and her mother's red and her father's brown one, hanging up in their usual places.

The same poster of a white house with a scarlet door, and a balcony with a table and two chairs, looking out towards a turquoise sea, hung in its frame on the wall opposite the bottom of the stairs. Sam remembered her mother buying it. They'd been on holiday in Greece, staying on an island the name of which Sam couldn't remember. Her mother had said it was the sort of house, in the sort of place, she'd like herself and Sam's father to grow old in.

They walked down the hallway and into the kitchen. Sitting there sipping coffee and eating great big, thick, slabs of toast smothered with peanut butter was a Sunday morning tradition. Especially if Sam had stayed out late on Saturday night – it would be the glue that stuck her sleep-deprived body back together again. But that happy, homely, lounging around, doing nothing in particular Sunday morning sort of smell, and all the memories that went with it, had been swallowed up by another that was far stronger and more insistent.

'Don't bother to put the chicken into the fridge. Just leave it out. I'll make that casserole. You must be starving. You haven't eaten anything since breakfast ...'

Sam slammed out of the kitchen and up the stairs. She ran along the landing and into her room. She threw herself down onto the bed. Her father was in hospital, lying there in the intensive care unit, hooked up to machines, and all her mother could talk about was food.

There was a knock.

'Sam?

The door opened.

'Are you all right?'

No, she wasn't.

'Shall I make you some tea?'

Tea was the last thing she wanted.

'I'm fine, just really tired. I'll come down later...'

The door closed.

She checked her mobile. The first message was from Katie asking if Sam was feeling better, that Leo really liked her and wanted to see her again. The next message was from Lou saying, in her own dreamy I'm-here-but-I'm-not-really-here sort of way, pretty much the same thing. The third was from Shelly and it was all about the boy at the fair, the short, stocky one who kept punching the air, what he'd said, what she'd said, what he'd done, what she'd done, on and on it went. Sam was about to turn the mobile off when she realised there was a fourth message, one she'd missed earlier:

"Sam. It's Dad. I don't know whether you'll get this message – suspect you're still in bed, fast asleep – which is where you should be at this time on a Sunday morning. Wish I was. But if you don't it doesn't matter because I'll ring you again as soon as I get to the airport. It's just that after what we talked about last night, about what Mum said, about me leaving, I just wanted to tell you that you really mustn't worry. It will be all right. We'll sort something out. Traffic's moving so I've got to go. Love you lots. Always have. Always will."

SEVENTEEN

ONE. TWO. PLEASE, NO, it couldn't be. Three. Four. The clock chimed five. But what clock? And where? Because there was no such clock in the house, there never had been. Sam hauled herself out of bed. Where was she? Everything was wrong. This wasn't her bedroom. The ceiling was too low and there was just one window. The floor was wooden and black rather than carpeted and brown. There was a fireplace instead of a radiator and just in front of her, where there should have been a door, there was a wall.

Her mind followed her legs over to a washstand. Her arms and hands poured water out of a jug into a bowl, picked up a rough cloth, soaked it in the lukewarm water and washed her face. They unbuttoned the top of her long-sleeved nightdress and, reaching down inside, gave each armpit a good scrub. They did the same between her legs. They dragged a comb through her hair and then tied it back in a ribbon.

A pile of clothes lay in a crumpled, unwashed heap on a rickety chair beside the bed. First one thick, black, wool stocking, then a second, was rolled up her leg and over her knee. Next were a pair of knickers that were so long and baggy they would have been too large for someone three times her size.

The nightdress she was wearing was tugged off and a sleeveless, knee-length slip pulled over her head. A corset was jerked up bit by bit over her hips until the top was digging into the skin below her breasts. She looked down, through

66

somebody else's eyes, powerless to stop what was happening, as her hands tightened the laces, forcing her chest out and her waist in.

Fingers she didn't recognise did up the ten buttons on the long-sleeved, floor length, brown dress. They tied an apron securely around her waist. Her feet slid themselves into a pair of lace-up, black leather ankle boots lying on the floor beside a chair.

Her hands straightened the bed and plumped up the pillow. Her feet walked her over to the door. Her right hand opened it. On the floor, directly outside the bedroom, was a glass jar. Inside the jar was a single white rose.

Sam opened her eyes. Her heartbeat slowed. She was inside her own body, in her own room and she was lying on her bed. The ceiling was not too low. There were two windows and brown carpet on the floor. And the door leading out onto the landing was exactly where it should be, on the other side of the room. And it was seven o'clock at night. Not five o'clock in the morning.

She'd definitely heard those chimes. But her mother had always refused to have a grandfather clock or anything similar; the constant chiming, on the hour, every hour, would keep them awake all night. And the chimes had sounded very distant. As though they were coming from a long way down in a much larger house, the sort of house that had attics, a basement and several floors. Not the modern, brick box type of house Sam and her parents lived in.

She slid off the bed and padded over to the window. The lights along the promenade always came on at sunset, as late as eight o'clock in the summer and as early as four o'clock in the winter. Today was Sunday, it was November, and the wind was howling in off the sea and there they were, twinkling away off into the distance, even though there was nobody around.

The first time she'd been at the fair, on the ghost train,

sitting in the cab with Leo. The second time, she'd been running down the road, trying to reach her father's car. She hadn't really thought about it, she'd been so worried about the accident, her father being in hospital, whether he would ever come home again, but now this slip into another world had happened again. And this time when she was asleep, in her bedroom, safe inside her own home.

She opened her bedroom door. There was no glass jar and no white rose. She padded down the landing. The door to her parents' bedroom was closed. She raised her hand to knock and then lowered it. She should let her mother rest.

She went on, slowly, down through the silent house. The rain started as she entered the kitchen, a single drop, then several, then a squall. She pulled down the blind and closed the curtains.

It could have been any other Sunday evening. The kitchen was filled with the smell of her mother's chicken casserole simmering in the oven. Apples, bananas and oranges were neatly stacked in the blue and white bowl her parents had brought back with them from Morocco and a bunch of lilies, pink ones, were sitting in a glass vase on top of the bookcase which contained her mother's constantly expanding collection of cookery books.

A bottle of red wine was sitting there, opened and only partly finished. She poured herself a glass. She took one sip. And then a second sip. There were some lettuce, tomatoes, cucumber and a packet of mixed peppers in the fridge. She would make a salad and then go upstairs and wake her mother.

She sliced up the green and then the red pepper. And she poured herself another glass of wine. She cut the cucumber into thick slices and then cut each individual slice into four. She poured herself a third glass of wine.

She couldn't remember drinking her very first glass of wine. It was probably on holiday, with her parents, perhaps when they were on one of their camping trips in France. And the glass had probably contained more water than wine. But she could definitely remember smoking her first cigarette. Her mother was out, and her father putting up some shelves downstairs, when she sneaked out of her bedroom, down the landing and into her parents' bedroom. She unzipped her mother's handbag. She searched through all the tissues, used and unused, the soggy chocolate bars and the crumpled up parking tickets and shopping receipts until she found a lighter and a packet of cigarettes.

She sneaked back down the hallway into her room. Sitting on the edge of the bed, with the door closed and the window wide open, she smoked first one, then two, then three. It was when Sam was smoking her sixth that she began to feel as if there was a cheese grater lodged inside her chest. She lit and then took a drag on the seventh. She stubbed it out. All she could taste, all she could smell, was cigarettes. They were in her hair, on her clothes; they were everywhere. There was no way either her mother or father, if they came into the bedroom, would not know, instantly, that she had been smoking.

She opened her bedroom door and crept down the corridor to her parents' bedroom. She unzipped the handbag, put the cigarettes back where she'd found them and then zipped the handbag shut. She crept back down the hallway into her bedroom. It still stank. And the mug she'd been using as an ashtray was full of cigarette stubs.

Back out into the hallway, this time into the bathroom. She closed the door, locked it and then emptied the stubs into the toilet. She flushed and then flushed again. The stubs were still there. She closed her eyes, flushed again and then opened her eyes. They were still there, bobbing up and down in the bottom of the toilet. Someone tried the door handle. There was a knock. A voice, her father's, asked if she was all right. She said nothing. He asked her to open the door. She did so.

He walked into the bathroom, glanced down at the toilet and then turned to look at her. And he laughed.

Her parents hadn't had an argument. No one had asked anyone to leave. Her mother and father were together and everything was going to be fine. It was somebody else's father, not her own, who was in the intensive care unit. In just a few minutes, her mother would walk into the room and they would sit, the two of them together, at the kitchen table. Her mother would scold her for drinking the wine and then pour a glass for herself.

The phone would ring, her mother would answer it and it would be her father saying that he was in his hotel room and he was missing them. Her mother would hand her the phone and he would ask her how she was and what had she done that day. She wouldn't tell him about the three glasses of wine she'd drunk. But he would guess – and he would laugh.

For a moment she believed her own lie. She heard footsteps on the stairs, the door opened and there was her mother. But then the feeling of control slipped away leaving her naked to the truth she had been trying so hard to avoid. Her mother was asleep upstairs and, she, Sam, was sitting, very alone and very drunk, at the kitchen table.

She walked out into the hallway, up the stairs and along the landing to her parents' bedroom. She knocked on the door, nothing, and knocked again, much louder, again nothing. She opened the door.

'Mum…'

She groped her way across the room.

'Mum?'

Her mother was lying, fully dressed, on top of the duvet. Her face was blotched and her eyes were puffy. In her hand was a scrunched up paper tissue. Several others lay scattered over the bed and on the floor. Sam stepped back.

What good would be done in waking her mother up? What

was the point in going over and over something which had already happened; even if her parents hadn't had the argument, her mother hadn't told her father to leave, he would still have left for the airport, the girl would still have walked out in front of his car and he would still be hooked up to machines in the intensive care unit. Nothing would be altered. Nothing would be changed.

She crept out of the bedroom, closing the door behind her. She crept back along the corridor, down the stairs and into the kitchen. She picked up the bottle of wine and emptied its contents, every single last drop, into her glass and opened a second bottle.

EIGHTEEN

May 1917

THE INSIDE OF THE compartment crashed to black. She screamed. And then it was daylight again. The train was still thundering on and the young soldier sitting next to her was smiling.

'Have to get used to 'em, love, tunnels, there's lots of 'em between here and London.'

Jess and her mother had always stopped to wave at the trains thundering past on the other side of the river, north to London and south to the coast. But she had never been on one, not until that morning.

She pushed her way into the carriage, along the corridor, into a compartment and down onto a seat. Outside, villages, fields and valleys were soon replaced by houses, chimneys and factories. And the colour of the countryside, the blue of the sky, the green of the fields, the pink of the blossom on the trees, was replaced by a dirty grey. The sky was grey. The houses were grey. Even the people were grey.

But Clapham Junction station wasn't grey: it was black. The air was full of soot and it smelt so bad it hurt to breathe. There were people everywhere, scurrying around like ants, going upstairs and downstairs, into tunnels and out of tunnels. The platforms went on and on, stretching off forever into the distance.

Jess stood there, holding tight onto her suitcase, doing exactly what her mother had told her to do; get off, stand on the platform, don't move, not to worry, the Major would soon find her. That had been half an hour ago. The train on which she had arrived had pulled out. A second one had pulled in and was already pulling out. And still there was no sign of the Major.

Jess took the letter her mother had given her out of her pocket. It was from the Major and his wife and printed on it, at the top, was an address: Eaton Villa, Glebe Road, London SW11. Her mother insisted that she should have it 'just in case'. Was 'just in case' waiting for half an hour on a platform with no sign of the Major? Had they forgotten her?

Her suitcase was getting heavy. Her mother had told her not to put it down; it would only get stolen. She put the case down and sat on it. If someone wanted to steal her case they would have to steal her too.

'Jessica? Jessica Brown?'

A big man, completely bald, arms swinging, was marching down the platform towards her.

'Explosion last night at a munitions factory in east London. Seventy-three dead, hundreds injured. They're still digging them out…'

The Major picked up her case and marched off. She ran behind him, along the platform, down a flight of steps and into a tunnel. More steps, another tunnel, and they were outside the station.

A car, if one came into the village, had been regarded as something to be kept well away from; you couldn't trust them not to explode. But now, right in front of where she was standing, there they were, hundreds of them crawling up and down the road like a mass of giant beetles.

She'd never seen anything like it. Cars and horses pulling carts, and strange-looking things which looked like very tall cars, with people sitting both inside and on top, were all jostling for space along a narrow stretch of road. And she'd never heard so much noise. At home, any travel or transport had always been done by horse and cart. The carts, like the ones here, had big iron-shod wheels but they'd made hardly a sound clip-clopping through muddy farmyards and down country lanes. But in London, those same iron-shod wheels going over stone cobbles made enough noise to waken the dead.

There was an angry honking of horns as the Major stepped off the kerb. He marched, weaving in and out of the traffic, without hesitating, towards the other side of the road. Jess stood there, frozen, as a car crawled by just inches from where she was standing. She took a deep breath and stepped off the kerb. A second car crawled past. A person was driving it, and there may well have been people sitting inside it, but all she could see was its shiny, polished metal.

She continued forward. The Major was alive and well, and still marching, and so was she. A large cart drawn by two horses, loaded up with barrels, rumbled towards her, sparks flying from its metal wheels. She should wait for it to pass. But the Major had already reached the pavement and was now striding off down the street. She walked out in front of the cart. If she hurried, didn't hesitate, she would make it. One step, two steps, but just as she'd reached the middle of the road, her feet slid out from underneath her.

She crashed down, face first, onto the wet cobblestones. The cart wasn't stopping. It wasn't even slowing down. She would be crushed to a pulp as the metal clad wheels rolled, without stopping, over her shattered bones.

A hand tugged at her arm. She was dragged her up onto her feet. She was pulled forward, out of the way of the cart, round the back of a car, round the front of a second car and up onto the pavement on the other side of the street. Before she could say thank you, the barefooted boy wearing the ragged remains of a red, grey and tartan waistcoat was back, darting in and out of the traffic, bucket in hand, scooping up horseshit.

She struggled to keep up, sweating inside the heavy coat, her new boots pinching, as the Major marched ahead. They passed a baker, a butcher, a tobacconist, a draper and a milliner. The baker and butcher had their shutters down. Other shops, although still open, had windows which had been boarded up.

The queues of people waiting to buy food back home in her village had been long but the queues they were walking past now, here in London, snaked out of the shop, along the street and round the corner. It was impossible to tell where one queue ended and another began. And no one was talking to anyone. The women were just standing there, hollow-eyed, sunken-faced, their shoulders drooping, one in front of the other, all dressed either in black or grey, waiting their turn.

A shopkeeper, sleeves rolled up, a long white apron tied round his waist, came out of a grocer's shop and said something she couldn't hear. The queue lurched forward. A group of women started shouting. Others started screaming. Two women prodded and poked him in the chest forcing him back, step by step, towards the doorway. A woman picked up a stone. She hurled it at the shop window. There was a loud crack, followed by silence, and then glass exploded out onto the street. Jess had heard talk, at home in the village, of food riots in the cities. Now she was seeing one.

'Fighting on the streets, next thing there'll be a revolution, like in Russia. Damned Bolsheviks…'

She followed the Major right into a narrow street. Houses were lined up, shoulder to shoulder, on both sides of the road. There was not an inch of space between them. The cottage where her family lived may have been poor, with only one room, but there was nobody, to their left, right or opposite, watching and listening to everything they were doing. And they had a garden, all planted up with vegetables, beans, onions and potatoes, and flowers, like her mother's blue cornflowers, and when you walked down the path, and out through the

75

gate, there were fields, and hedgerows and trees. Not grey stone and red brick.

At the end, facing directly towards them, was a tall building, also red brick. The roof had fallen in. All the windows had been blown out and the walls, the ones that still remained, looked as though they were about to collapse. A child's boot lay abandoned amongst the broken glass and brick dust covering the ground. The Major stopped. He pulled a handkerchief out of his pocket.

'There was an air raid. The teachers took the children down to the basement, to the infants' classroom, where they would be safe. The bomb went straight through the roof, into the empty boys' classroom, down through the empty girls' classroom, and into the infants' classroom where all the teachers and children were sheltering.'

The Major blew on his nose long and hard.

'Eighteen dead, more than a hundred injured.'

The war had always been in France. But now it was happening here at home. The white plane, with the black crosses painted on the underside of its wings; she now understood why her father had ordered her back to the cottage. But a thatched roof and mud walls wouldn't be much protection if one, single bomb could rip apart a solid, brick-built building like this.

The Major stuffed the handkerchief back in his pocket. He picked up her suitcase and marched off. She followed him down more streets lined with houses; Ebbs Road, Honeywell Road, right into Hillier Road and then, finally, left into Glebe Road.

She stared up at the Major's house. Eaton Villa was like nothing she'd seen before. With its soaring turrets, pointed arches and snarling stone lions, it looked more like a church than a family home.

'My wife's never recovered from losing our two oldest boys.'

The Major put his key in the lock.

'To lose them both within a month of each other, both in the fighting in France, was just too much. It broke her heart.'

The Major turned the key. The door opened.

'The house is too large for just the two of us and with no help it has been difficult to keep things as we would like. Getting the letter from your mother was a blessing.'

She followed the Major into the hallway. She stopped, her mouth open, staring up in astonishment, at the vaulted ceiling, the jewel-coloured tiled floor and the glowing wood-panelled walls. The house, from the outside, looked like a church. Inside, it was a castle.

NINETEEN

'You pick up the receiver and you say, "The Osborne household."'

Jess had heard about telephones. She knew they existed, like she knew India and elephants and tigers existed in some far distant land, but she had never expected to find herself living in a house that actually had one.

'We have gas down in the kitchen, but in the main part of the house, where the family live…'

The Major's wife clicked a switch. The hallway was flooded with light.

'We also have electricity, whenever we want, day or night.'

Her father had called her mother his 'Little Sparrow'. She had brown hair and brown eyes, was shorter than most women, and used to be, what her father described with a wicked smile and a glint in the eye, well-rounded. She also never stopped moving, hopping and pecking, from one job to the next: washing, cleaning, cooking, working hard, day and night, to look after her family.

But if Jess' mother had been her father's 'Little Sparrow' then the Major's wife would have to be her husband's 'Big, Fat Chicken'. Or even 'Big, Fat Turkey'. Jess had never seen a woman so large. And it wasn't just her body. It was the clothes, the yards and yards of heavy black material trimmed with lace, the skirts and underskirts and petticoats, and who knows what else, sweeping up the staircase behind her.

'In other houses, it is usual for maids to turn and face the wall whenever a member of the family passes by. But here, in our smaller, more relaxed household, keeping your eyes down and not speaking unless spoken to will be perfectly acceptable.'

The first landing was lit by a narrow stained-glass window. An enormous pot, containing a small tree, stood to the left of a table covered with a tapestry rug. A heavy, carved wooden chair sat on either side.

'The main bedroom, the Major's dressing room and this...'

The Major's wife opened a third door. A trough, as wide as it was tall, stood on what looked like clawed feet in the centre of a large, white tiled room.

'You put the plug in the hole, like this, carefully, so you don't scratch the enamel, and then you turn on the taps. The right hand one is for hot water. The left one is for cold water.'

When her father had been at home, and there had been enough money to buy coal to light a really good fire, they'd had a bath every month. Her father would draw up four or five buckets of water from the well. Her mother would heat it in a large, black metal cooking pot over the fire. When it was hot, but not boiling, her mother and father would lift the pot off the range and pour the water into the hipbath. Her father would be the first in, then her mother, then Jess and, finally, her baby brother. It had to be in and out, really fast, if the last person into the bath was to get any hot water.

The Major's wife opened a fourth door. It was another white-tiled room. But this one was much smaller and it contained a throne-like seat.

'You lift up the lid and you sit down. And when you have finished you pull this.'

The Major's wife tugged on the chain hanging from the metal box high up on the wall.

'Not too hard – you don't want to break it.'

There was a loud clanking. Water gushed and swirled down into the toilet.

'Don't forget to put down the lid. The Major is very particular about his lid.'

At home, they'd had a privy at the bottom of the garden. Outside it looked pretty, all covered with honeysuckle and roses. But, inside, however often her mother swept and however hard she scrubbed, and however often the waste was emptied, it always smelt. But here, at Eaton Villa, there were no smells; all the waste was washed away, in pipes going down, through and then underneath the house.

At home, they'd had to clean themselves up with whatever they could get hold of, scraps of old newspaper, sometimes handfuls of hay. But here there was a special box, attached to the tiles on the wall, containing sheets of hard, shiny paper.

'You buy it at the shops – Bronco – we must never run out.'

They were now on the top floor of the main part of the house.

'This was Peter's bedroom. And this was William's.'

The drawing room, the dining room, even the main bedroom, were all crammed with pictures and ornaments. She'd never seen so many bits and pieces. There was not an inch of space that wasn't covered with some bit of china or glass. But these two rooms, at the top of the house, were empty except for a bed, unmade, a wardrobe and a chair. Anything that could possibly hold a memory had been stripped out.

'And this is Tom's...'

The third and smallest bedroom was different. It had pictures and books and there was a pile of shirts, ironed and neatly folded, lying on a bed made up with sheets, blankets and pillows.

'And this is the nursery...'

White walls, a table, four chairs, three of them child-sized, two cupboards, a guard in front of the fire and bars securely fixed at the windows.

'When Tom, our youngest son is back from France, he'll get married and start a family and the house will go back to being the happy home it used to be…'

Hills she was used to climbing but not stairs. And the next flight was very narrow and very steep. Another door and they were standing in a low-ceilinged, narrow corridor running under the length of the roof.

'This is where all the servants slept. As well as your mother we had a cook, Mrs Johnson, and a scullery maid, Mary, and a nursemaid, Lucy.'

They stopped outside a door at the end of the attic corridor.

'This was your mother's room.'

It had a sloping ceiling and a window tucked away under the eaves. There was a narrow, iron bed with a cotton coverlet, a wardrobe, a wooden chest and a washstand with a bowl and jug. A strip of carpet partly covered the black-painted wooden floorboards.

'Put on this brown working dress and apron when you get up in the morning. You wear it when you're doing the dirty work. You will need to get most of that done, lighting the range, laying the fires, before you serve breakfast. You put on the black dress and the white cap and apron before serving lunch. There's two of each, one on and one for the wash, and there's another black dress for best. You will find some underwear, two vests, two pairs of knickers, two pairs of stockings and a corset, in the chest.'

She'd only had one dress at home although you could hardly call it that. It had two sleeves and a hole for her neck and it was made up of patches taken from her mother's old clothes all sewn together. And now she had five dresses, all clean and new and crisp, hanging up on hangers in her very own wardrobe. They'd never had money for underclothes, vests or knickers, you just went without, but now she had both, two of each, and two pairs of stockings and a corset.

A book lay on the bed.

'Study this carefully, in detail, in the evenings once your work is done. Mrs Beeton will tell you everything you need to know in order to fulfil your duties efficiently.'

It was nearly as thick as the family bible her mother kept on the mantelpiece at home.

'Unpack and change and then come straight down to the kitchen. The Major likes dinner to be served prompt at eight o'clock. Not a minute later.'

The door closed. Jess sat on the edge of the bed. She bounced up and down. She turned back the coverlet. A pillow, a lower sheet, an upper sheet and not one but two blankets, both clean.

She opened the book:

"Chapter One. As with the commander of an army, or the leader of an enterprise, so is it with the mistress of the house. Her spirit will be seen through the whole establishment; and just in proportion as she performs her duties intelligently and thoroughly, so will her domestics follow in her path. Of all those acquirements, which more particularly belong to the feminine character, there are none which take a higher rank, in our estimation, than such as enter into a knowledge of household duties; for on these are perpetually dependent the happiness, comfort and well-being of a family…"

And so it went on for over five hundred pages.

She knelt up on the bed, unlocked, and then slid open the window. Seeing the towers, steeples, roofs and chimney pots disappearing off into the distance, the same view her mother must have seen when she slept in the same room, perhaps in the same bed, she allowed herself to believe that she did have some chance of happiness in this new and better life.

'I'm Ellie. Who are you?'

A snub-nosed girl, wearing a maid's black dress, a white cap perched on top of a mop of frizzy, black hair, was leaning out of the attic window of the next-door house.

'I'm Jess.'

'So what are you – stupid or desperate? You've got to be one or the other to be a maid-of-all-work…'

A deep thump vibrated across the rooftops. The glass in the window above Jess' head rattled. Clouds of pigeons flew up into the air. A second and a third thump followed. There was silence and then it started up again, repeating itself, on and on, until the individual thumps had joined up to become one, long, continuous, moaning roar. Whether it was coming from down inside the earth or from up in the sky, it was impossible to tell – it was everywhere.

'What's that?'

Ellie snorted.

'Needs must when the devil drives.'

Her head disappeared back inside. The window slammed shut.

TWENTY

June 1917

"*The general servant, or maid-of-all-work, is perhaps the only one of her class deserving of commiseration: her life is a solitary one, and, in some places, her work is never done.*"

She'd got up at five o'clock, but already, just two hours into her day, she was running out of time. She'd only been at Eaton Villa for six weeks but each night, when she finally crawled up the stairs to her bed, her back ached so much she thought it would break. Her cracked and bleeding hands were so bruised from carrying coal, cleaning grates, turning mattresses, washing windows, wiping down floors, sweeping carpets, dusting china, polishing glass and scrubbing sheets that she could no longer feel them. Her new home was nothing more than a prison. And she, its only servant, the maid-of-all-work, slaving eighteen hours a day, seven days a week, was its prisoner.

"*The general servant's duties commence by opening the shutters (and windows, if the weather permits) of all the lower apartments in the house; she should then brush up her kitchen-range, light the fire, clear away the ashes, clean the hearth, and polish with a leather the bright parts of the range, doing all as rapidly and as vigorously as possible, that no more time be wasted than is necessary. After putting on the kettle, she should then proceed to the dining room to get it in order for breakfast.*"

Upstairs, the Major's wife enjoyed showing off the house's newly-installed electricity to her guests. But downstairs nothing had changed. The Improved Leamington Kitchener had always been a monster – and still was a monster. Jess stepped forward.

'If you want a fight, I'll give you a fight,'
The monster glowered at her.
'Close this one down…'
It belched out a huge cloud of soot black smoke.
'Open this one up.'
It gave out a long, deep, angry whistle.
'A bit more coal.'
A jet of blisteringly hot steam narrowly missed hitting Jess in the eye.

However hard she tried to obey the Major's wife's instructions, however much or however little coal she put in, whatever valve she closed or opened, somehow she never quite got it right. The range had been there when Jess' mother had first arrived to work at the house. That was well over twenty years ago. The hot plate; the roaster with moveable shelves, which could be turned into an oven; the double dripping-pan; the flat grid irons for cooking chops and steaks; the ash-pan; the meat-stand; and the large metal boiler with a brass tap and a steam-pipe had been the Major's wife's pride and joy. Right now it looked and sounded as if it was about to explode.

Jess took the plate down off the pantry shelf. There were two rashers of bacon and two eggs leftover from yesterday. The cheese soufflé that forgot to rise, the mayonnaise that curdled, the blancmange that collapsed into a heap; the list of her culinary failures went on and on. The first time she made salad cream, following Mrs Beeton word for word, the Major's wife had called her away from the kitchen, to help sort out the laundry. When she returned she put in sugar, double the amount, instead of salt. The Major had sent back her mushroom soup saying it was lumpy. Yes, she'd sieved it, but she'd used the wrong sieve – the one made out of metal rather than hair. Whose hair she didn't know, she didn't even want to think about it. But, unlike the salad cream, the mushroom soup had been edible.

Jess shivered. The dining room was a cold and depressing place even on a June morning but this was where the Major and his wife ate their breakfast, an egg or a rasher of bacon, sometimes a mushroom or even a tomato, on a slice of toast, so it was always the first room to be cleaned.

"Nothing annoys a particular mistress so much as to find, when she comes downstairs, different articles of furniture looking as if they had never been dusted."

She laid out an old sheet on the floor in front of the fireplace. Back, at home, the same leaves were used to make tea, again and again, for over a week. At Eaton Villa, leaves, even ones that were just a day old, were kept, but not to make tea. Instead, they were scattered over the contents of a fireplace before brushing the ash out of the grate.

On her first morning she'd followed all the instructions on Mrs Beeton's long list – except this one. Three hours later, when the Major and his wife came down to breakfast, they had found every mirror, picture frame, ornament, trinket and box – and there were hundreds of them scattered over every available surface – covered in coal dust. It had taken Jess most of the rest of the day to wash, dust and polish the room and all its contents back to normal. She had never made the same mistake again.

She'd buffed the marble fireplace, laid the fire, and rubbed and rubbed the grate, over and over again, until it was gleaming. Now it was time to sweep over the Major's beloved Indian carpet. The first time she'd crawled underneath the dining room table, she'd knelt there, dustpan and brush in hand, entranced by the richly robed huntsmen on their long-legged horses galloping across the carpet's jewel-coloured plain.

But the huntsmen and the horses, which she had so loved and admired and had found so beautiful, had quickly, within just days, become things to be dreaded, even hated. Because however long and hard she brushed, however badly her back ached, however bruised her knees, the Major would always find, each and every morning, a speck of dust that had been missed. And if a single strand of the silk fringe, which edged all four sides of the carpet, hadn't been combed out and wasn't lying straight, there would be all hell to pay. An almost impossible task given the wooden parquet floor was so slippery.

The brass carriage clock on the mantelpiece chimed the half hour. She crawled out from under the table. There was always one, often two, sometimes three clocks in every room, and, hour after hour, upon the hour, the half hour and the quarter hour, they chimed out their orders. And as the day got longer, and she became slower, the faster the clocks chimed.

"The hall must now be swept, the mats shaken, the door-step cleaned, and any brass knockers or handles polished with leather."

She picked up the hearthrug in front of the fireplace and carried it out into the hall. She threw it down beside the front door. The mats and rugs in the hallway would have to wait until after she'd taken the Major and his wife up their morning tea.

Jess slid the heavy bolts back off the front door. She opened it and stepped outside. She'd polished the brass knocker a couple of days ago but it had already begun to tarnish. It would have to be cleaned again or the Major would have something to say. The mix of linseed oil and brick dust was hard on the hands but not as hard as the cleaning soda she had to use for scrubbing out the lead-lined sink down in the kitchen. And the steps leading up to the front door would have to be washed and then rubbed down with the block of hearthstone cleaner. White wasn't enough. They had to be whiter than white. If the Major and his wife had their way she would be spending the rest of her life down on her knees.

The two cotton pads, which were now stitched into the insides of her stockings, had helped. But there was no such protection for her hands. At the end of her first day at Eaton Villa, she'd collapsed down, exhausted, on her bed in the room at the top of the house, and had woken up, five hours later, lying there, fully clothed, the coverlet stained with blood from her bleeding hands.

She shook out the hearthrug and then paused. She stood there, eyes closed, face upturned, breathing in the air, dragging it into her body, lungful by lungful. She couldn't hear the guns out in France, the wind was blowing in the wrong direction, but she could still sense them. The same way you could sense a storm coming. A quiver in the air, a gust of wind, a flash of lightning and then thunder would crack through the sky.

But, if you could hear the guns here in London, what must it be like in France? Serving as a soldier out there on the Western Front, as her own father had done, having to live with the thunder of those guns, day after day, night after night; a continuous barrage of sound right over your head, the earth shuddering under your feet, seeing your friends and colleagues being blown apart? It was too terrible to imagine.

A clock chimed, then another, calling her back into the house. Jess stepped inside. She pulled the heavy front door shut behind her. She went back down the hall and into the dining room. She laid the hearthrug out on the wooden parquet floor in front of the fireplace.

She was working unpaid, just for her bed and board with one afternoon off a month, as she had no previous experience. But the Major and his wife had promised her mother that they would give her a reference. And a reference was what she needed in order to apply for a paid job. But for how long, how many days and hours would she have to work, to slave, before she got that reference?

Her mother had been in service but that didn't mean she had to be. Once she was sixteen there was nothing to stop her handing in her notice. With the men gone, it was the women who were now working on the land and in the factories: jobs that paid well. No one wanted to be a servant, the hours were too long and the pay was too bad. Which was why the Major and his wife had taken her on; they had been desperate.

But she knew what her mother would say. She was lucky. She wasn't cold and she wasn't starving. What more could she, or should she, want? And her mother would have been right. So she would stay where she was – at least for the moment.

"The servant should now wash her hands and face, put on a clean white apron, and be ready for her mistress when she comes downstairs…"

She froze. A loud and insistent knock hammered into her head like a nail being hammered into the lid of a coffin. It was too early for a delivery but not too early for a telegram.

'Jess. Open the door.'

The Major was standing on the landing, his wife clinging to his arm. Both were still in their nightclothes.

'But…'

'Do as I say. Open the door.'

She willed whoever was standing out there to go away, to find another house, another family to rip apart. It had happened to her family, to herself and her mother. And it had already happened to this family, twice, and it couldn't happen again. The pain would be too great. They had no more men to give.

She opened the door. A blonde-haired young man, dressed in military uniform, turned to face her. His eyes were the same piercing, bright blue as the cornflowers in her mother's patch of garden.

TWENTY-ONE

'Has he looked at you? Really, and I mean really, looked at you?'

The youngest son had been home for two whole days and Ellie had talked of nothing else.

'Now come on, Jess, has he?'

The shopping list the Major's wife had given Jess that morning had been double its usual length. While the one and only surviving son was home on leave he would want for nothing.

'I don't know. How would I? I'm not allowed to raise my eyes from the floor...'

'But Jess, there are ways...'

Ellie lowered her head and keeping her gaze down to the pavement slid her eyes sideways.

'You'll get stuck, Eleanor Baxter, when the wind changes...'

It was what her mother used to say whenever she caught Jess sticking out her tongue.

'Being all prim and proper, Jessica Brown, will get you nowhere. There aren't enough men to go round. I'd go with a chimney sweep if he'd have me...'

Ellie slid her eyes to the left.

'But even if they tell you they want to walk you up the aisle, put a ring on your finger, take no notice, they'll still want to sample the goods first. So you just have to get yourself in there, get yourself in the family way and then you'll be looked after. It's the only way to keep them. The nearer the bone, the sweeter the meat...'

Standing right in front of them, propped up on a crutch, hand outstretched, was a skeletally thin boy dressed in filthy rags. At the end of his left leg, where there should have been a foot, there was a mangled mess of shattered bone.

He must have slipped, in the middle of the traffic, exactly as she had done. But nobody had seen. Or if they had seen, they had just turned and walked away, leaving the boy lying there, helpless, as the cart, its iron-clad wheels sparking, rumbled towards him.

Because it was the same boy, she was sure of it, the one she'd seen darting in and out of the traffic, so confidently, so quickly, outside the station the day she'd arrived in London. The boy who had taken her hand, pulled her up from where she had fallen and who led her to the safety of the pavement on the other side of the street. He was still wearing the red, grey and black tartan waistcoat, but it was so matted with dirt, so ripped and torn, it was barely recognisable.

There had been a longer than usual queue at the bakers that morning. When, after over an hour, it had been her turn to be served there had been just one solitary loaf left on the shelf.

She took the bread out of her shopping basket and walked over to the boy.

'Jess? What are you doing?'

He had saved her life. She couldn't save his, that was impossible, but she had to do something.

The boy's eyes widened. He took the bread, hugging it to his chest and then turned and limped away towards an alleyway. He stopped and looked back, the crutch wedged under his arm. Jess nodded her head, so slight but still a nod.

'He's seen you, that Tom, the Major's son. He's right there, outside the house. He'll have you for stealing…'

And Ellie was off, running down the street, her shopping basket in her hand. And Jess was left standing there, eyes down, staring at the pavement, as the youngest son walked towards her. She was fifteen and his mother's maid-of-all-work. He was twenty and the son of the house. She washed and ironed his clothes, cooked and served his meals, cleaned his room and made his bed.

'Why did you give that boy the bread?'

He was a young man with an old man's voice. Its tone and depth had surprised her that first morning, standing there at the front door, eyes down and invisible, as he strode past her into the house to greet his parents.

'Is giving a loaf to a starving boy something to be punished?'

And except for a quick nod of the head or a curt, 'Thank you,' she had, since then, continued to be the silent and invisible servant – until now.

'Some might call it stealing. Others might call it charity.'

Head held high, she strode off towards the house.

'Jess, where have you been?

His mother was waiting for her in the hallway.

'Why has it taken you so long?'

The Major's wife never went out shopping. Which was why she didn't understand that Jess had to queue not at one shop but several, often three or four, if she had any chance of getting at least some of the items on the list the Major's wife gave her each morning.

Sometimes, after she'd been shuffling slowly forward for nearly an hour, the shopkeeper would come outside and pull down the shutters. There was nothing more inside the shop to sell. And then Jess and all the other women and children, lined up in front and behind her, would have to find another shop and join another queue.

Her first day in London, following the Major home from the station, she hadn't understood what had driven the women to rioting. But now she did. She was young and fit, and could stand there for hours, but for the elderly or sick it was impossible. Desperate people throw stones.

'Did you get everything?'

'Yes, ma'am.'

That she came home with anything was a miracle.

'The jam and the eggs...'

Her mother had made her own jam from the strawberries and the raspberries she grew in their garden. And her father would often come home carrying some newly laid eggs, still warm with white and brown fluffy feathers stuck to them, as part-payment for the work he had done that day. But here in the city everything had to be paid for with pennies and shillings. The cost of the spoonful of jam and the two eggs she'd managed to buy that morning would have kept her own family fed for a month.

'Yes, ma'am.'

The Major's wife clapped her hands.

'The beef?'

Whether it was beef, or cat, or dog, or even rat, the Major's wife had some meat for her suet pudding.

'Yes, ma'am.'

'And the bread, you did get the bread?'

What should she say? Should she tell the truth, that she'd bought the bread but had given it away to a starving boy who would be lucky if he lived another day?

'I'm sorry, ma'am.'

'What? There must have been a loaf of bread somewhere...'

'I'm sorry, ma'am. The shops had run out.'

'All the shops?'

If there had been one more person standing ahead of her in the queue, her lie would be the truth.

'Yes, ma'am.'

'We'll have to get you out of the house a little earlier tomorrow morning...'

Eyes down, mouth closed, Jess followed the Major's wife along the hallway.

'Tom is out with his father. They won't be back until five o'clock, possibly six o'clock, which will give us time to get ready. The glass and china will have to be washed and the silver will need polishing. The Major wants flowers, candles, everything just like it used to be...'

Her last day at Eaton Villa was going to be a long, hard one. After the son told his parents about their maid, a thief and insolent with it, she would get her dismissal. She would go back home to the country and try to find a job, one that didn't need a reference, perhaps in a factory or on a farm, closer to her mother.

'Jess, I forgot, this came in the post for you.'

She tucked the envelope up her sleeve. It must be from her mother. The paper, the envelope and the stamps would have been expensive. And she would have had to find someone to write it for her. She must have something very special to say.

TWENTY-TWO

SAM TIPPED HERSELF OFF the chair. The floor lurched over to one side. Walls that had been solid tilted and swayed. She grabbed hold of the table and closed her eyes. The darkness whirled and swirled. She opened her eyes and raised her head. The window seemed much further away but also much larger, soaring over the kitchen and everything in it, including herself.

She fixed her eyes on the curtains. The spots and stripes, which before had been so regimented and orderly, now shimmered and shook, spiralling and cart-wheeling, backwards and forwards, out of control. Finger by finger, she detached herself from the table. She slid her foot out across the floor. It held. One step, two steps, a third step and she was safely across.

She leant over the kitchen sink, fighting the waves of sickness bubbling up inside her. The feeling of well-being she had experienced earlier had been replaced by a cold, dark, bleak emptiness. She was drunk. And not just drunk but very drunk. And she had to get upstairs to her bedroom without her mother either seeing or hearing her.

She turned off the light and, with her hand clamped onto the doorframe, took one step and then another out of the kitchen into the hall. She listened for movement, a door opening, the pad of feet along the landing, but none came. Her mother was still in her bedroom and, hopefully, still asleep. She clicked off the light.

Halfway up, the staircase slid away from underneath her

feet and she collapsed down in a heap. It was comfortable, very comfortable, just lying there, going nowhere and doing nothing. She closed her eyes. The house started to spin round, faster and faster. The spinning slowed and then stopped.

She looked down towards the hall. She looked up towards the landing. Both seemed a very long way away but if she went up it would, at least, be in the right direction for her bedroom. And if she stayed down on her hands and knees there would be less risk of falling.

She pushed herself away from the wall and up and around onto her knees. She planted the point of one elbow and then a second elbow into the carpet. She hauled one knee and then a second knee up onto the first step, second step, and on and on up, until she hauled the last knee up and over the final step. She glued her back up against the wall and, inch by inch, straightened her legs until she was standing upright. She edged her way along the wall, down the landing.

Somebody was standing underneath the street lamp on the opposite side of the road. It was too dark to be able to tell whether they were male or female, young or old. But to stand there in the pouring rain with no umbrella, staring up at the house, was more than a little strange.

Sam pulled the curtains tight shut. She tumbled, almost falling headlong, down the stairs. She grabbed the key off the hook, jammed it into the lock and turned. The top bolt, the bottom bolt, if somebody wanted to come in they would have to batter the door down.

She put the key back onto its hook and then hauled her shaking body, step by shaky step, the floor and walls rocking and rolling around her, up towards the landing. She clamped her hands over her mouth. She ran past the closed door of her parents' bedroom and threw herself into the bathroom. She leant over the sink, heaving and retching, while her body emptied itself of red wine. She picked up her toothbrush. Yes, she would feel better if she cleaned her teeth but it would have to wait. She was just too exhausted.

She slid out of the bathroom, along the landing, hugging the wall behind her. Her mother coming out of her bedroom and finding Sam collapsed in a comatose heap just wasn't worth thinking about. Walking or crawling, she had to get to the safety of her bedroom.

But was it safe? Downstairs in the kitchen, she had been so drunk, so out of it, slumped there head down on the table, she wouldn't have heard somebody stealing into the house. Anyone could have slipped the lock on the front door, crept down the hall, up the stairs and along the landing into her bedroom.

She pushed open the door and flicked on the lights. Her laptop was still on her desk, her mobile on the top of the cupboard beside the bed. Her rucksack lay on the floor, the side pocket un-zipped, her purse easy to see and grab, just as she had left it.

But perhaps they didn't want her laptop or her mobile? Or her money, what little there was of it? Perhaps they wanted something else? Perhaps they were outside, on the balcony, waiting for her? Because what they wanted was...

She was drunk, and she was tired, and she was scaring herself witless about nothing at all. No one was outside. Nobody was waiting for her. It was just another stupid, silly, drunken, little thought.

She checked the door out onto the balcony, not once, but twice, unlocking it, re-locking it, and then, just in case, checked again for a third time. She pulled off her shoes, pulled off her clothes, pulled on her pyjamas, crawled underneath the duvet and turned off the light.

TWENTY-THREE

FOUR HOURS' SLEEP WASN'T enough. And definitely not enough if you've drunk more than a bottle and a half of red wine.

Her head, her arms, her legs, were as heavy as lead. Her tongue felt like sandpaper. She dragged herself out of bed, across the room and out of the door. It was grey and misty outside. And it was raining – the sort of slow, steady, stubborn drizzle which would go on and on throughout the rest of the day.

She shuffled down the landing and into the bathroom. She brushed her teeth and gargled with mouthwash. At least she no longer smelt or tasted of sick.

She'd spent most of the night, huddled under the duvet, afraid that if she closed her eyes and went to sleep she'd be woken up by the chiming of a clock. And when that clock chimed, and when she woke up, she'd find herself inside somebody else's body, in a room that didn't exist, putting on clothes that didn't exist.

She closed her eyes. She opened her eyes. Sam Foster was still there, staring back at her out of the bathroom mirror, even if she did look just a little bit hungover. And just a little bit crazy.

The door to her parents' room was open. The bed was made but not in her mother's usual I-don't-know-why-I'm-bothering-to-do-this-it's-all-so-boring sort of way. Pillows and cushions were lined up in a perfect line, rather than thrown together in a haphazard pile, and the duvet was positioned exactly in the middle of the bed rather than hunched over to one side. Neat and orderly, everything precisely in its place, the bedroom looked exactly how her father would have left it. Not her mother. Or at least not the mother she'd had yesterday or the day before yesterday.

'They're doing tests…'

Her mother, her phone glued to ear, was pacing up and down and around the kitchen. It must be somebody from work. Not the hospital. Which wasn't good news, her father's condition hadn't improved, but then it wasn't bad news either. There had been no change for the worse.

'We should know later this morning…'

She didn't know which was scariest; the mother who had gone to bed and cried herself to sleep or this mother, this too brisk, too bright and too organised one, chatting away on her mobile.

'We have to be at the hospital at ten…'

Sam took a mug out of the cupboard and poured herself a coffee. She took a sip. It was hot, too hot, but it numbed the dull ache inside her head.

'They'll have the results of the scan by then…'

The evidence was there for all to see; two wine bottles, both empty, on the floor beside the rubbish bin. Her mother must have found them exactly where Sam had left them last night, sitting on the table, when she came downstairs to the kitchen earlier that morning.

'I'll give you a ring…'

Would she say something, about going to her room and staying there, leaving Sam all alone to get drunk as a skunk? Or would she sweep it to one side, pretend that everything was as it should be, that nothing out of the ordinary had happened?

She took another sip of coffee. All she wanted to do was crawl back into bed and bury herself under the duvet. But that wasn't an option.

The doorbell rang, loud and long.

Parked in the road, at the front of the house, was her father's car. Sam ran out into the hall. The front door wouldn't open. She tried again. It wouldn't budge. And then she remembered.

Looking down through the upstairs window and seeing the person, man, woman or child, it was impossible to tell it was so dark, standing outside in the pouring rain, staring up at the house. But last night she had been so drunk she would have seen, and believed, anything. She slipped the bolts back, took the key off the hook and unlocked the door.

'Hello, Sam. Your dad phoned us yesterday. We've fixed the seatbelt…'

It was the man from the local garage. It had been silly to hope, even for just a second, it was her father. She'd been there, sitting behind him in the car, when he made the call.

'Hello, Mr. Harris.'

Her mother, smiling as if this morning was just another Monday morning, was walking towards them down the hallway.

'All right, there is it, Mrs. Foster, at the front, or shall I put it round the side?'

'It's fine. Thank you.'

The man held out a set of keys. Her mother took them.

'Cheers.'

He walked away down the path.

'I phoned your school. They're not expecting you until after lunch…'

A girl, dressed in black, was standing underneath the streetlamp, on the other side of the road, directly opposite the house.

'There's some toast but you'll have to be fast…'

And she was looking at Sam; not just looking, she was staring.

TWENTY-FOUR

THEY STEPPED OUT OF the lift. Outside, on the street, there had been laughter and sunlight. But here, on the very top floor of the hospital, in this windowless dungeon of a corridor, if someone had told her that the world had come to an end, that she and her mother were the only two people left alive, she would have believed them.

'Mrs Foster. Sam.'

A man, as tall as he was broad, with skin as black as the uniform he was wearing was white, was walking down the corridor towards them.

'My name is Mac. How are you doing?'

A fluorescent light cracked and fizzed overhead.

'The consultant's office is at the bottom of the corridor, Mrs Foster, second door on the right. They're waiting for you.'

He put his hand on Sam's shoulder.

'What do you say to the two of us going in to see your father?'

Yesterday afternoon, when her father was transferred from the accident and emergency department to the intensive care unit, she and her mother must have come up in this same lift. But she could remember almost nothing about the ward itself and nothing at all about how they had got up there.

'If you would prefer we could go to the family room and wait for your mother there. We have one right next-door to the ward. Have a coffee or some tea? It's your call.'

It had to be faced.

'I'd like to see Dad.'

'Follow me, Sam.'

They went through the first set of double doors, then a second.

'You OK?'

'Yes, I'm fine.'

Her memory of the ward, the people in it, what they had been doing, was all wrong. What she'd been expecting, and dreading, was gloomy darkness with doctors and nurses walking from bed to bed talking in hushed whispers. But this space was brightly lit, like a supermarket, and filled with people, some in uniform, but many not, clustered around a central desk, talking on phones and tapping at computers.

'When a patient is very sick or heavily sedated we have to use a ventilator to assist them with their breathing…'

She followed Mac down a central corridor lined on either side with cubicles. To her left, lying on a bed, hooked up to a bank of machines, head bandaged and with an oxygen mask over their face, was a person. Man or woman, young or old, it was impossible to tell. A nurse, lifted her head, nodded and smiled, and then turned back to the syringe she was filling.

'We use monitors, each bed has its own set, to keep an eye on heart rate and rhythm, blood pressure, blood oxygen level, respiratory rate and temperature. And then there are the pumps, or syringe drivers, which help administer fluids and drugs. There are probably more than a hundred machines in here. Each has an alarm. And they all sound different. There's one now…'

Loud and angry, and impossible to ignore.

'There's nothing to worry about. It's usually just telling us that something needs checking…'

They turned right into the last cubicle. And there was her father.

'Here, Sam, why don't you sit down.'

And what had seemed, just a second ago, perfectly possible was now the most difficult thing in the world. He sat down beside her.

'You know, many of the patients who come in here do get better. Some who were so sick their families thought they would never return home. But they did. We had one lady who was in a coma for six months. When she woke up she didn't know she'd been in a road accident. She thought she'd been waiting to board a flight to America to see her family for Christmas...'

An airport, that's where her father would go, inside his head, if he was in a coma. Only he'd never been that good at waiting.

'There's always hope. However, small and far away that hope may seem. And it's that hope which will help your father and which will help you and your mother help us to help him. Hope. And love. And those two things are almost as important, perhaps even more important, than any of the drugs, or nursing and medical skills that anyone, here on the ward, can provide.'

If only she could believe him.

'Would you like to take your father's hand? That way he'll know that you're here, sitting beside him...'

The antiseptic, straight-lined, fluorescent whiteness of the hospital ward was replaced by a low-ceilinged, oak-beamed room with sagging cob walls and a beaten mud floor. The only light came from a single candle fluttering on a low table beside a bed, which was made out of wood rather than metal. The person lying on the bed, on a coarse woollen blanket, thrown over a lumpy, grey mattress, shiny with grease, was not her father but a child. It was a boy, his eyes were closed, and he was naked. Lying beside him was a very small, white coffin.

'What are you frightened of?'

A woman stepped forward out of the darkness. The dress she was wearing was so thick with dirt it was impossible to tell whether it was brown, blue, black or grey. Hair hung in limp, tangled strands round and over a face that was so thin, so pinched, it looked as though it was collapsing in on itself.

'Send him on his way...'

The woman stepped towards the bed. She lifted the boy, so pale, so still, so small, he could have been a doll.

'You loved him when he was alive...'

She kissed the boy's forehead and then turned towards Sam.

'Now love him when he's dead...'

Sam didn't know where she was. She didn't recognise the woman. Nor did she recognise the child. But what she did know was that he was dead and this woman was expecting her to lean forward, take him in her arms, to embrace him, even love him. Her mind fought, tried to pull away, break itself free, as her head bowed down.

She was warm rather than cold. And the smell of dirt had been replaced by the smell of chemical cleanliness. She was back in the hospital.

'I can't.'

'Why? Are you frightened?'

The white hand, punctured with tubes, lying on top of the sheet, was the same hand, the same blood and bones and skin that had saved her life. It had pulled her out of the river, when she'd fallen into the water just above the weir and was about to drown.

'No. I don't know. Perhaps...'

But she couldn't touch it. It was impossible.

'Sam, we've had many people like you, who've said, or thought, felt, the same thing. It's no big deal. But, you know, whatever you think, your father will know that you're holding his hand. He will sense it and it will help him get better...'

All she wanted was to get up out of this chair and out of this place, stuck between the world of the living and the world of the dead, a place with no hope and no future, as quickly as possible.

'But what if he doesn't get better? What if he dies?'

It was out. She'd said it. She'd almost screamed it.

Mac took her hand. He held it tight.

'Follow me.'

TWENTY-FIVE

June 1917

THE FIRST COURSE HAD been served and cleared, there had been no complaints, and now the Major, his wife and their son were eating their beef-steak and kidney pudding. Or even cat-steak and kidney pudding. Jess took her mother's letter out of her apron pocket. There was a tinkle of a handbell from the dining room. Let them wait. Twenty seconds wouldn't kill them.

She'd washed all the glass, got the Prince of Wales' soup on – turnips, scooped out into balls, and then boiled in stock – and made the pastry for the bakewell tart when the Major's wife came down to the kitchen to insist that Jess iron the napkins for a second time.

And then the silver cutlery, which had already been cleaned and polished, had to be cleaned and polished again. Then the roses were too short, the lilacs too tall and the delphiniums too blue. And the knives weren't lined up straight, the wine glasses were all wrong and the damask tablecloth wasn't white enough. She'd had to clear the table, search out another tablecloth, and then lay everything out, all the silver, the glass, the candles, the flowers, all over again. And so it went on all through the morning, the afternoon and into the early evening.

Just when she thought that everything that could be done had been done, the Major's wife spotted a grease stain on the dining room carpet. What stain? Because thirty minutes later, and three trips up and down to the kitchen, the carpet looked exactly the same.

And, now, upstairs in the dining room, sitting at the perfectly laid table, with the candles flickering and the silver glinting, the son was telling his mother about her thief of a servant. But it didn't matter. Tomorrow she would be gone. The Major's wife's hands wouldn't be quite so lily-white after she'd stripped the sheets, turned the mattresses, cleaned the grates, brushed down the carpets and scrubbed the saucepans.

Jess tore open the envelope, read the letter and then folded it once, twice, three times, before tucking it back up her sleeve.

She slid, eyes fixed firmly on the floor, through the doorway into the dining room.

'How can I expect my men to do their duty, to go out there and die, when the country they're supposed to be dying for doesn't give a damn. They come to me, men twice my age, with wives and children, a family to keep, to ask for help, to see if I can do anything and there is nothing I can do...'

The Major put down his glass.

'Tom, please...'

He picked up the decanter of wine.

'There has always been and will always be the rich and the poor, the fortunate and the less fortunate.'

He filled his glass.

'That's how it is.'

She darted in and out clearing dirty dishes and cutlery.

'And, to "do your duty", for something, a way of life you believe in, that you hold dear to your heart, is an honour...'

She leant forward to take the son's plate.

'Honour?'

His hand slammed down. She jumped back. A tear splashed down onto the table.

'There's nothing honourable in being herded over the top like animals being sent to the slaughter, to be ordered to walk directly into the fire of a German machine gun, and to be left screaming in agony, ripped to pieces, hanging on the barbed wire, begging for someone, for your best mate, to put a bullet in your–'

'Tom, that's enough.'

The son closed his hand into a fist.

'While the folks back home, your masters and betters, are sitting comfortably, smugly dining on their Prince of Wales' soup and their beef-steak and kidney pudding followed by bakewell tart with custard, your children are dependent on the kindness of a passing stranger for a husk of bread. That's not "society". At least not a society, a way of life, a set of so-called civilised rules that I or my men either believe in or are prepared to die for…'

The son picked up his plate. His hands were trembling.

'Thank you, Jess.'

She took it.

'Ah, Jess.'

Was this her dismissal? Until a few minutes ago, until she'd read the letter, it had been something to look forward to. Now it was something to dread.

'Yes, ma'am.'

She bobbed a curtsy.

'Your letter, from your mother, how is she? Well I hope?'

Please don't let the Major's wife see that she was crying.

'Yes, ma'am, very well.'

Jess bobbed a curtsey.

'I've set the fire in the parlour, ma'am …'

She ran from the room, wiping the tears from her eyes, her mind following her body, up the stairs, to the first floor of the house. She pulled down blinds, closed curtains, turned back bedclothes. She then went up the stairs to the second floor and along the corridor, pulling down blinds and closing curtains in the nursery and the two empty bedrooms until she reached the youngest son's room.

A notebook was lying open on top of the bed, and, on a

page of that notebook, there was a pencil sketch of a girl. She was so alive, so real, Jess half expected her to walk off the page and out into the room. She looked up and caught a reflection of herself in the mirror over the fireplace. The girl in the notebook stared back.

TWENTY-SIX

SHE WAS STANDING THERE, on the bridge, looking down at the river below. And then she jumped. The water closed in over her head and she was sinking down, down and down. Strands of weed entwined themselves around her arms and legs. She clawed at it, fighting to free herself, but the weed's vice-like grip only tightened, pulling her down, down and further down into the black depths below. She gasped and gulped. Water, not air, filled her lungs.

'Wake up, Jess, wake up.'

It had been a dream, a nightmare, nothing more. She was in the cottage, with her mother and father and her baby brother, and it was a hot summer's morning. She could already feel the heat of the sun on her skin. They were going to walk, the four of them, along the path that led through the meadows down to the river for a picnic.

'Wake up, Jess'

She jerked upright. She wasn't with her mother and father by the river. She was in the basement of the Major's house and, standing opposite her, on the other side of the table, was the Major's son.

'I'm sorry…'

She pushed her aching body up out of the chair.

'Would you like some coffee, sir?'

'No. Thank you.'

He was here to dismiss her.

'Your parents…'

'They've gone to bed.'

The gaslights on the wall flickered, rising and falling, twice in quick succession.

'What's that?'

'It's a warning, sir, to expect an air raid.'

The range was piled high with dirty dishes. It would take her half the night to scrub, wash, dry and put them away. And then she would have to get the range stoked up and the copper filled ready for the morning. But it was a job that had to be done if she was going to try and get the Major and his wife to agree to keep her on.

'Where do we go? Is there a shelter?'

'Your father refuses to take notice of them, the raids, sir.'

'But, Jess, you don't have–'

'And he insists that everyone else in the house does the same.'

Whatever the son of the house had to say, why didn't he just say it, get it over with and then go upstairs to his bed and leave her alone to get on with her work.

'But what about you?'

She was more tired than frightened. At least if a bomb came she would get some rest – even if it was the sort of rest you never woke up from.

'If it's going to hit you, then it will hit you. And there's nothing you can do about it. It's nature's way, that's what my father always said…'

'Your father? Where is he now?'

A game was being played; he was the cat and she was the mouse, and she had no choice other than to go along with it.

'He's dead, died in France, nearly three months ago now, sir,'

'I'm sorry, Jess, that was thoughtless of me. My father mentioned it, in a letter, when he told me that your mother had written asking if you could come here…'

A plane hummed overhead.

'Sir, about the bread and what I said, I'll make it up. I'll work extra hours…'

She had to convince him.

'I'll do anything, anything at all to keep my place here. Sir, I'll do extra–'

'My name's Tom. And there's nothing to make up. You did the right thing giving that boy the bread. You just never gave me a chance to say it. Jess, look at me…'

She kept her eyes to the floor.

'Look at me, please, that's an order.'

She raised her head.

'Please, sit.'

It was another order but the way it was said made it something else. They sat, together but apart, on opposite sides of the table.

'Jess, upstairs, you were crying. You were trying to hide it from my mother but I could see. Please tell me what has upset you so much.'

She wanted to talk but could she trust him?

'Our local vicar wrote to me…'

She pulled the letter out of her sleeve.

'He got this address from the letter your parents sent to my mother offering me the job here. He found it in the cottage…'

She put it down on the table between them.

'My mother's dead. She killed herself…'

A woman in a neighbouring village, back at home, lost not only her husband but also her two sons out in France. She hanged herself from the roof beam inside her cottage. Jess overheard her mother whispering to her father that it was an offence before God and that the woman would go to hell. And now she had done the same thing herself.

'Do you know how it happened?'

His voice was very quiet, very controlled. It was also kind.

'Her body was found in the river.'

Whether her mother had just waded in, her pockets filled with stones, or had thrown herself off the bridge, she didn't know. But she guessed it must have been at or near to the bridge where the river flowed over the weir before turning, deep and fast, out towards the sea. But what she couldn't guess was how her mother must have felt. That terrible choice that she'd had to make, in those seconds, before she threw herself off the bridge.

'People who kill themselves go to hell. That's where my mother is. In hell–'

'No, Jess, she's not in hell. It's the people left behind, who stood there watching, listening to the cries for help, without doing anything, they are the ones who go to hell, a hell of their own making, filled with fear and guilt, not the people who are–'

'I did what I could. I didn't have any money. If I had I would have sent it...'

Was it a sudden decision, made in a moment of desperation? Or had her mother known all along, from the moment she wrote the letter to the Major and his wife, and then sent Jess away into service, exactly what she was going to do.

'She knew that. You know that. You must never feel guilty. She was a good wife, a good mother, to you and your brother, and to me, much more so than my own mother, when I was a very young boy, growing up in this house. A kind, brave, generous woman, who deserves peace, not punishment.'

Peace could be the signing of treaties and the silencing of guns or the certainty that when you went to bed at night you would still be alive to wake up the next morning.

'When are you going back?'

But peace wasn't only about the end of war – it was having a roof over your head and food on your plate and knowing that the people you love would always return.

'To France? Perhaps tomorrow, perhaps next week, I really don't know. When the telephone call comes, that's it, I have to go.'

'What you said, about the guns, the wire, the bullet in the head. My father, did he die like that?'

'Don't think about how he died, Jess. Just remember how he lived. Think about the good times, the two of you, you and your father, had together.'

Something stirred inside her. Was it hope? And, if it was hope, hope for what?

TWENTY-SEVEN

THEY CLEARED THE DINING room and then washed and dried the glasses, the decanters, the china and the cutlery. Standing, side by side, they scrubbed, dried and polished the saucepans before hanging them back on the hooks above the range. When they talked it was a whisper, a question, an answer, a word here and there.

And now the clocks were chiming two o'clock and all that could be done had been done; everything had been put away, either on shelves or in cupboards, the kitchen sink and table scrubbed, the floor swept and wiped down, the range stoked up and the copper filled.

'Go and get some sleep, Jess, you must be exhausted...'

She turned off the gas lamps, lit a candle, and then, together, she in front, he following behind, they climbed the narrow stairs from the basement up to the ground floor of the house. They slid the bolts across the front door, switched off the electric lights and then walked together, side by side, the candle flickering, up the wide, wood-panelled staircase towards the first floor landing.

A floorboard creaked. The Major was a heavy sleeper; the two double whiskies he had after dinner guaranteed that. But, over breakfast, the Major's wife would complain that her husband's snoring had kept her awake, tossing and turning through most of the night, until, exhausted, she fell into a deep sleep just as Jess arrived with their morning tea. They waited, nothing, the Major snored on.

They continued on up to the second floor. Eyes down, she bobbed a curtsey and turned to walk away. She had one more flight of stairs to climb. His hand slipped into her hand, gently pulling her back.

'Jess, you will always have a home here.'

His fingertips slid over her fingertips.

'For however long you want it…'

And they parted. Tom, the son of the house, to his bedroom, squeezed between the bedrooms of his two dead brothers. And Jess, the maid-of-all-work, up the stairs to her room in the attic where her mother, now her dead mother, had once slept.

She'd left the window open when she got up that morning, over twenty hours ago now, but the room was still unbearably hot. She stripped off her clothes and threw them down on the chair. She pulled on her nightdress and blew out the candle. She lay down on top of the bed and looked up, out of the window, at the stars in the night sky.

This room, this house, the people in it and Ellie next-door were all she had. There was no one else. No brothers, no sisters, nobody. She was quite alone. Everyone she had ever loved, her father, her brother, and now her mother, was gone. She would never see them again.

But she still had a job, food on her plate and a roof over head, and she owed all that to her mother – and Tom. He had said nothing to his parents about what had happened, her rudeness and the loaf of bread she had given away, that morning.

Just under three hours later, as the clocks started to chime five o'clock, she dragged herself off the bed, stumbled over to the washstand, poured water out of the jug into a bowl, picked up the cloth, soaked it and washed her face. She unbuttoned the top of the long-sleeved nightdress and, reaching down inside, gave each armpit a good scrub. She did the same between her legs. She dragged a comb through her hair and then tied it back in a ribbon.

Her clothes lay in a crumpled heap on the rickety chair beside the bed where she'd thrown them the night before. She rolled first one thick, black, wool stocking, then a second, up her leg and over her knee. She pulled on her knickers, took off her nightdress and then tugged the slip over her head. She stepped into the corset, jerking it up, bit by bit, over her hips until the metal stays were digging into the skin beneath her breasts. She tightened the laces, forcing her chest out and her waist in, and then knotted and tied them together in a bow.

The long-sleeved brown dress had ten buttons. She did them up, one by one. She tied the floor-length apron securely around her waist and then slid her feet, one at a time, into the lace-up, black leather ankle books lying on the floor next to the chair.

She straightened the sheet and blanket, plumped up the pillow, and walked over to the door. She opened it. The narrow, low-ceilinged, windowless corridor, running along the length of the attics, normally smelt of sweat and dust, of mould and mildew. Today it was filled with the scent of roses.

She looked down. On the floor, directly outside her bedroom door, was a glass jar. Inside the jar was a single white rose. She leant down. She picked it up and carried it into her room. She placed it on the chair beside her bed.

When Tom had insisted on helping her to clear up last night, downstairs in the kitchen, he was just being kind. But going out into the garden, picking the rose, putting it in the jar, and then creeping through the house up to the attic, in the middle of the night, to put it outside her bedroom door, was something altogether different.

Back home, in her village, it would only have meant one thing. Her parents would have smiled and, when she asked them, would have agreed that she and the boy could walk out together. But, up here in London, working as a servant in the Major's house, there was a line between those who lived upstairs and those who worked downstairs. And that line should never be crossed, not by anyone, whether master or servant.

That day, and the day after, when the master's son walked into a room, she walked out of it. When she had to ladle out his soup or pour over his gravy, she kept her eyes firmly down. But the harder she worked at ignoring him, the harder he worked at getting her attention.

She'd never ever seen or eaten a chocolate. But there they were one morning when she came down to the kitchen, three of them, nestled up together on a plate in the larder. And beside them was an envelope with her name written in ink on the front. It was from the Major's son. The chocolates were a gift. And could she, please, eat them quickly before they melted away in the summer heat.

All through the day, every time she went into the larder, she stared at them. Should she? Shouldn't she? Was eating a chocolate, a gift from her employer's son, crossing the line?

That evening, at dinner, after she'd cleared the main course and taken the dirty plates and cutlery down to the kitchen, she opened the larder and took out the chocolates. She carried them upstairs and placed them in the centre of the dining table.

'Jess, what a surprise, chocolates, my favourites, wherever did they come from?'

She bobbed a curtsey, keeping her eyes down, and said nothing. The Major's wife turned to her son.

'Tom? Is this you? How lovely. The last time I had a chocolate was before the war.'

The Major's son picked up the plate.

'Granaches of strawberry with rum, hazelnut praline or crème mocca?'

'The strawberry, it's my favourite, so clever of you to remember…'

Jess turned towards the door. She would leave the family, upstairs, eating their chocolates while she went, downstairs, to get on with the washing up.

'Father?'

'The hazelnut praline. Delicious, Tom, thank you.'

The Major's son pushed back his chair.

'Which leaves the crème mocca for you, Jess.'

He was walking towards her.

'And I won't take no for an answer.'

She stared down at the single chocolate sitting on the plate.

'Jess?'

She turned and ran out of the door, along the hallway and down the stairs into the basement. Right or wrong, whether the Major's son was just being kind, or whether he had some other motive, she could have said, 'Sorry but I don't like chocolate,' even if it was a lie. But, instead, she'd run out of the dining room without a curtsey; enough in most houses to get an instant dismissal.

The next morning, at breakfast, everything was as usual. No mention was made of what had happened the evening before. She served the family their poached eggs on toast, went upstairs, made the beds and opened the windows to air the rooms. She cleared the table, did the washing up and gulped down a piece of toast and a mug of lukewarm tea. The Major's wife gave her that day's shopping list and then left, with her husband, to go out on a call. They would not be back until after lunch.

Raindrops were splattering down on the pavement when she opened the front door. It was just a summer shower, the sort that would stop as quickly as it had started, but heavy enough to do some damage. The Major and his wife would not be pleased if they came home to find their curtains and carpets soaked through.

She went back into the house. She closed the front door and climbed the stairs to the first floor. She closed and bolted the windows. She climbed up the stairs to the second floor. She'd presumed that the Major's son had gone out, alone or with his parents. She walked down the hallway. She was wrong. His bedroom door, usually open, was closed.

TWENTY-EIGHT

THERE WAS AN INTERCOM to the right of the door. Mac pushed the button. There was silence and then a crackle.

'Hello.'

Where was he taking her? This was more like a prison than a hospital.

'Hi, it's Mac.'

'Hi, Mac. Come on in.'

There was a buzz and the doors hissed open.

'I come here every day. To remind myself...'

Water cascaded over a cliff face down into a fern-edged pool below. A mother monkey, cuddling a baby monkey to its chest, dangled from a tree. A snake, curled round a bunch of bananas, slept on, a smile on its reptilian face. Frogs with orange webbed feet sat, red eyes bulging, on enormous, table-size, lily-pads. Parrots darted from tropical flower to tropical flower.

Mac reached a finger out towards a cloud of yellow and green butterflies shimmering in the sunshine. There was a buzz. A door opened.

'The special baby unit.'

On all four walls and across the ceiling, shoals of rainbow-coloured fish swam through glimmering coral. There was no thumping on keyboards, no barking out of orders or crashing and slamming of doors. It was so quiet, so peaceful, that the special baby unit, and everybody in it, might well have been swimming along the bottom of the ocean floor.

'Many of the babies that come here are pretty close to the edge…'

Two people, a man and a woman, were sitting beside a clear plastic box the size of a microwave. It was surrounded on all sides by row upon row of machines.

'The little girl, inside the incubator, is Ruby. Ruby was born at twenty-three weeks, seventeen weeks premature. She's been here, in the special baby unit, for two weeks now…'

The wrinkled lump covered in tubes, with a huge head and tummy and skinny arms and legs, looked more like a premature alien from outer space, an infantile ET, than a human baby.

'No one thought she would get this far. But she's a real little fighter. She never gives up. If anyone's going to get there she will.'

The man put his arm round the woman's shoulder. He hugged her close.

'It may be weeks, even months, before Ruby goes home. She's so young she hasn't even got ears, they haven't had time to grow, but they'll come.'

The couple leant forward, heads together.

'Sophie and Daniel come in every day. They sit with Ruby, they tell her stories, sing to her, paint her pictures, even play her music. Very young babies, even as young as Ruby, always know when someone's there…'

The next bed in the ward was a cot, the sort you would expect to see in any home where there was a very young baby, and it wasn't surrounded by machinery.

'Noah was premature, exactly like Ruby. At the beginning nobody knew whether he would get through the next minute or hour, let alone day or week…'

A man and a woman were standing, arms entwined, looking down at the baby. And this one did look like a baby, the sort you see in TV adverts crawling around with an angelic, beaming smile on its chubby, pink face.

'There were days, very early on, when Noah was so sick, he couldn't breathe, he couldn't feed, his whole body was yellow with jaundice. Emma and Jake would go back home to bed not knowing, when they woke up in the morning, whether they would still have a son. But they never stopped hoping. And they never stopped loving.'

The baby gurgled.

'Today's a special day, for everyone, the nurses and doctors here in the unit who've been looking after him, but especially for Noah's mum and dad. Because, today, Emma and Jake are going to do something they never thought they would be able to do...'

The woman lifted the baby up out of the cot.

'They're taking Noah home.'

Ahead was another cot and lying in that cot was another baby. But that was it. There were no parents, no mother and father, just one nurse. She looked up as they approached.

'Hi, Mac.'

'Sam, this is Jennie. She's in charge of the ward. Jennie, this is Sam.'

'Hi, Sam.'

Jennie tucked a blanket round the sleeping baby.

'How is she?'

'Doing fine. But we're keeping her here, just to keep an eye on her.'

'And the mother?'

Jennie shook her head. 'Nothing.'

A phone started to ring.

'Too many babies, not enough beds. Bye, Sam.'

The little girl lay there, eyes tight shut, hands balled into fists, fast asleep.

'She was found on Sunday, early morning, in a bag, in the car park at the back of the hospital...'

Sunday, yesterday, the same day her father had been admitted to hospital.

'We got a phone call telling us where to find her…'

A hand uncurled.

'It was raining but the bag was watertight and she'd been wrapped up in a towel which had kept her warm. But we're worried about the mother. The police are trying to find her. Not to charge her, just to get her here to the hospital so she can be looked after, get some medical care. She sounded not much more than a child herself.'

The baby wriggled and burped, then opened its eyes.

'Has she got a name?'

'Not that we know of. There was nothing left with her, no note, nothing.'

The baby smiled up at Sam.

Light was replaced by darkness, the warmth of the hospital by the cold of a churchyard. She was sitting on a hard stone floor, her back against a wooden door, and something was tugging at her. She looked down – the something was a baby. It was feeding from her breast, a breast swollen with milk, which had to mean that it was her child. In the sense that the body she was inside had had sex with a man, the baby's father, had carried it for nine months, and given birth to it. She, her mind, had no memory of it, none at all. But what she did have, could feel, was a sense of connection to, even love for this tiny scrap of flesh, blood and bone.

Her eyes fluttered, closed, opened and then closed. All she wanted to do was sleep. She couldn't. She didn't know why, only that she couldn't. There was something else she had to do.

She eased the baby away from her breast and laid it, wrapped in its blanket, down on the floor. She hauled herself up. She buttoned her dress, then her coat and walked out of the porch into the churchyard. The body she was inside kept on walking down the gravel path while her mind, trapped inside that body, was shouting, 'Don't walk away, go back, you must go back, if you leave your baby she will die.'

'If the police can't find the mother, she'll have to go up for adoption.'

She was back in the special baby unit, standing beside Mac, surrounded by bleeping machinery. Seconds before, she'd been sitting in the church porch, the cold creeping up her body, with the baby tugging at her breast. It hadn't been her imagination, she hadn't been asleep so it wasn't a dream and she hadn't been drunk. On both occasions, in the intensive care unit and down here in the baby unit, she had been here in the hospital. And these slips into this other world, into this other girl's body, had been minutes, rather than hours, or even days, apart.

TWENTY-NINE

DRIVING ALONG IN HER mother's car, looking out of the window at the old lady walking her little snub-nosed, black-faced, curly-tailed dog; the two mothers chatting over their coffee, both tenderly stroking their eight-months-pregnant stomachs; the boyfriend and girlfriend entwined around each other at the bus-stop. It was impossible to believe that the uncomplicated world beyond that pane of glass, with everyone going about their daily lives, actually existed. Everything was so normal. Everybody looked so happy.

'There's no point you hanging around at home. There's nothing you can do. It will just make things worse. Dad's OK, he's stable, all we can do now is wait…'

That's what the young doctor with the stethoscope slung round his neck had said, standing by her father's bed, his arms neatly folded, in the intensive care unit. But there had been no smile on his face, nothing, not even a glimmer.

'You'll be better off here, at your school, with your friends.'

Sam unclicked her seatbelt.

'Keeping busy.'

Perhaps her mother was right. What would she do if she went back home? Go upstairs to her room, lie down on the bed, listen to her father's voicemail, cry herself to sleep, slip into another world, see and hear things that didn't exist, wake up, go downstairs to the kitchen and crack open and gulp down another bottle of wine? Then she'd go back upstairs and lie there all night too afraid to close her eyes, get up the next morning, her hands shaking, head throbbing, her body aching, desperate to go back to bed. And on and on it would go, round and round. She had to break that circle.

'I saw things, at the fair, and when Dad was driving away. But I'm not just seeing them, it's like I'm there, like I'm somebody else, living their life, walking down the street, wearing their –'

'I shouldn't have left you alone, Sam. It was wrong of me. I was just so upset...'

'Nothing happened last night. Not with the wine. It was before, when I woke up, in my room, and this morning, when I was with Dad and when Mac took me–'

'Sam, you're tired, you're upset and you're hungover. Now go in and see your friends. I'll see you after school. I'll ring if I hear anything from the hospital.'

It had been stupid to even try. She got out of the car, threw her rucksack over her shoulder, walked through the gate and kept on going across the tarmac towards the main school building.

She turned and tried to wave a wave that said, 'I'm fine, stop worrying, you can go now.' She expected, wanted, her mother to drive off but she didn't. Instead she waved back.

Sam waved again, turned, and continued towards the entrance and kept on walking until she'd reached the top of the steps. She stopped and turned. Her mother pulled out and drove away down the road.

She pushed the door open and walked through into the ground floor corridor of the main school building.

'Do you remember the one with the dead girl crawling out of the television...'

And there they were, her gang, huddled together under the oak tree at the edge of the football field. In the summer they would lie on the grass, sipping cold drinks and nibbling on carrot sticks and lettuce leaves, Italian 'designer' sunglasses, bought from a stall in the market at a tenth of the price of the real thing, perched on the tips of their meticulously freckle-free noses. On a grey winter's day they would shuffle, shivering, from foot to booted foot, muffled up in their coats and scarves, sipping coffee and chewing on pizza.

'And the one when the wife's trying to crawl through the bathroom window and her husband grabs hold of her legs and he tries to eat her. And when she gets out, through the window, there are all these dead people waiting. And she has to shoot them in the head because if she doesn't, and they bite her, then she'll turn into a zombie…'

Lou had seen them all – the originals and the re-makes. A red-eyed, hollow-cheeked, bloody-mouthed decomposing corpse, dragging its rotting limbs out of a coffin, was just about the only thing that could turn her on.

'Sam, where've you been? Did you get my message?'

Katie, the organiser of all organisers, who hated being ignored, was eyeing her up and down.

'Why didn't you phone me back?'

The last time she'd seen Katie, Lou and Shelly was at the fair on Saturday. It had been yesterday afternoon, Sunday, when she checked her messages.

'My dad's in hospital. He had an accident in his car, on his way to work…'

It felt like thirty years.

'He's in the intensive care unit, unconscious, hooked up to machines…'

Lou and Shelly were staring at her as if she, Sam, the best friend they went to school, out shopping and clubbing with, had just turned into one of the living dead.

'It's the fireworks tonight. We've arranged to meet the guys down there.'

Hadn't Katie heard?

'Not tonight.'

'Leo will be there.'

Didn't she understand?

'I've just said. Not tonight.'

'He's a nice guy, Sam. Loads of girls think he's more than nice. You're going to have to try harder if you want to–'

She was standing under the oak tree, at the edge of the football field, a place where she should feel safe, with Katie, Lou and Shelly. But the friends that she loved, and had spent so much time with, were now like aliens from another planet.

'My dad's in hospital, he's so sick he might even die, and the only thing you can talk about, only thing you can think about, is boys.'

She turned and ran across the playing field, along the ground floor corridor, through the entrance doors, down the steps, across the tarmac and out onto the street.

THIRTY

June 1917

SHE'D SEEN AND HEARD her mother cry and the other women in the village: when there was no money left to buy food, not even a farthing; when a son or daughter died; or when they opened the front door to find the post boy standing there holding out the letter every wife and mother dreaded. But the sound coming from the Major's son's bedroom was something much deeper, more painful, so filled with despair that it was impossible to believe any human bearing could survive such pain.

She was a maid-of-all-work. Whatever was going on behind that door was none of her business. She should just walk away. He was the Major's son; a soldier home from the front, he could look after himself.

But something had changed. The line had been crossed. Because now she wasn't just the maid-of-all-work and the boy behind that door wasn't just the Major's son. She was Jess and he was Tom, the same Tom who had looked after her, comforted her, shown her kindness after her mother had died. Who had told her she would always have a home, here in this house, as long as she wanted one.

Shouldn't she now show some kindness?

She knocked, a quick, double tap. She waited. She tapped again. Nothing. She turned and walked away. The young man's weeping followed her down the landing. She stopped at the top of the staircase.

He had said that night, down in the kitchen sitting together at the table, that her mother had been a brave and generous woman. Jess knew exactly what such a woman would do now.

She walked back along the landing, knocked and, without waiting, opened the door, walked across the room, reached up and pulled down the window.

The Major's son was lying face down on the bed.

'Sir?'

She placed a hand on his shoulder.

'Sir, it's me, Jess…'

His shirt was soaked through with sweat.

'Do you want me to call out a doctor?'

The weeping stopped.

'I don't need a doctor.'

'Are you sure? I can easily–'

He sat up on the bed.

'It's very kind of you but no, no thank you, I'm fine.'

'Looking the way you do, doing what you're doing, isn't fine.'

She sat down beside him.

'If my mother was here she'd want to know what was up, because something is for sure. But my mother's not here, you've just got me, so tell me, Tom.'

'No, Jess, I can't, you think you want to know but you–'

'Tell me.'

She said nothing, just waited, listening to the rain beating against the window.

'William and Peter, my brothers, lasted six months. They were killed within just a few weeks of each other. Peter by a sniper, a bullet through his brain. William leading his men over the top. They were hit by machine-gun fire. His sergeant managed to drag him back to the trench but he died on his way to the dressing station. I've been out there over a year now, in France fighting on the front line. Junior officers don't usually last longer than three months, four if they're lucky, many of them less than six weeks…'

He closed his eyes.

'At school, being part of the Officers' Training Corps had all been a jolly good game. And when the war broke out, joining up, serving your country and being a soldier was regarded as an extension of that game…'

She mustn't ask any questions. She mustn't say anything. She must just let him talk.

'When I was old enough to fight, Father organised a commission for me in his old regiment. He'd done the same for my brothers, both still out in France, and it was accepted, and expected, that he would do the same for me. And I had no quarrel with that. It was a war that was justified, a battle that had to be fought. The evening before I was due to embark Father took me out to his club. We smoked too many cigars and drank too many brandies. He told me how very proud he was. In the morning both of them, Mother and Father, came to the station. The train pulled out, the military brass band played and handkerchiefs were waved. But nobody, nobody at all, not my father, not my brothers when they came home on leave, had ever talked about the fighting… what it would be like…'

He reached out and took her hand.

'First time across no-man's-land, nothing big, no major push, a daylight raid, just myself and a handful of my men, checking out who was there, what they were doing. We cut the wire and crawled down into the enemy trench. I was expecting hell, machine-gun fire, bayonets, grenades, the full works, but there was nothing. It was empty. There was nobody there.

I sent my men ahead. I was about to follow, when there was this sound behind me. I don't know where he'd come from but there he was, this German, just a boy, standing rifle up, bayonet ready. He took a step forward and he stabbed at me. I fired my pistol but the wretched thing jammed. He stabbed again. I stepped aside, back against the trench wall, kicked out, knocked him down onto the ground and twisted the rifle out of his hand. I stood over him, looking down at a boy just like me lying there, helpless. I jammed the bayonet down into stomach and turned it, just like I'd been taught. He reached out towards me, tried to say something and I jammed the bayonet in deeper…'

His hand tightened its grip on hers. He shuddered.

'He was lying there, this enemy I had been told to hate, bleeding his guts out. And all I wanted was for him to push the bayonet aside, stand up, laugh, slap me on the back and tell me it was just a game, a fake, just like the ones we'd had at summer school. But no one was going to stand up because he was dead. The first man I'd killed was just a blonde, blue-eyed boy like me, who happened to be speaking the wrong language and wearing the wrong uniform. A boy who had a father and a mother and a brother and a sister, and all he wanted was to live, be happy, fall in love and one day marry and have a family. That's all my brothers ever wanted. And that's all I've ever wanted. To live and be happy and fall in love…'

He opened his eyes and turned and looked at her. And he was still looking as he untied her cap, unknotted her apron, unbuttoned her dress, unlaced her corset and removed, one by one, the pins from her hair.

THIRTY-ONE

She bobbed a curtsey.

'Ma'am.'

The Major's wife looked up from the letter she was writing.

'Yes, Jess?'

'Will that be all, ma'am?'

She put down her pen.

'Jess, I know it's the second Wednesday of the month but are you sure you can't delay your afternoon off? It's very inconvenient with Tom being at home. There's so much to do…'

Jess kept her eyes fixed to the floor.

'Ma'am, like I said yesterday, a friend's coming up from Sussex. We're having tea. I can't change it now, she'll already be on the train. The meat's done, ready to go on…'

Please don't let the Major's wife change her mind.

'The potatoes are peeled and the carrots…'

The Major's wife picked up her pen.

'Very well, you may go but make sure you're back by six o'clock. Not a minute later.'

She pulled off her uniform. She mopped herself all over with a damp cloth and slipped on the dress that Tom had smuggled into the house the day before. She brushed her hair, tied it back in a ribbon and then perched the straw hat, decorated with a bunch of roses, on top of her head.

She stepped out of the cool, dark kitchen into the baking

heat of the paved yard. She locked the door behind her. Up a flight of stone steps and she was in the main part of the garden.

The Major was at his club and his wife was resting upstairs, something she always did after lunch. The bedroom faced out onto the street, which was why she and Tom had agreed that Jess should leave through the back garden. If the Major's wife saw her wearing the dress questions would be asked. It was simple, pink roses on a white background but still beyond anything that Jess would ever be able to afford.

She ran across the lawn, unbolted the gate and slipped out into the alley, which ran along the back of the house. Two minutes later she turned left onto the main street. Forty minutes later she got off the bus at Kensington Gardens.

'Jess…'

He pulled her close.

'The shop assistant, she didn't believe me, not for a second, when I said I had to buy clothes for my sister…'

Two elderly ladies, tightly corseted in black from head to toe, swivelled their heads in Tom and Jess' direction.

'Tom, don't…'

She pushed him away.

'What's the matter?'

One old lady said something to the other old lady.

'People are watching.'

They both shook their heads.

'If they don't like it they can look the other way…'

The old ladies walked on, their backs straight, noses in the air.

'Jess, we have so little time.'

He pulled her closer.

'Promise me we'll be happy…'

You should never make a promise unless you could keep it.

'I promise.'

Tom's face relaxed into a smile.

'I thought we might go out on the lake. It will be cooler out there…'

He led her along a wooden pontoon lined on either side with rowing boats. Each had a number painted on its prow.

'This is ours. Number seven…'

She hitched up the skirt of her dress and, taking hold of Tom's hand, stepped into the boat.

'Sit yourself there, where I can see you.'

She did as she was told. He untied the boat.

'I'll get us out and then you can have a go.'

He sat down facing her.

'You have to keep the oars just above the water…'

He pushed off from the pontoon.

'Now you reach all the way forward. Make sure the blades are flat. Twist your wrist towards you, lower the blades into the water, keeping them perpendicular…'

They were moving away from the shore, fast, towards the centre of the lake.

'…Lift the oars, again keeping them flat, twist your wrists forward…'

There was a roar of laughter, followed by a loud bellow and a splash.

One young man was already in and the other three were stripping off their clothes. Another splash and two heads were bobbing in the water.

Tom pulled off his shoes, then his socks.

'Tom, what you doing?'

'What do you think…'

He stood up. He pulled off his shirt.

'You can't.'

'I can and I will.' He leant forward. 'And nobody, least of all you, Jessica Brown,' he kissed her, 'is going to stop me.'

He kicked off his trousers and dived in. Grinning, he swam

back to the boat, hauled himself up and hooked his elbows over the side.

'Coming in?'

'Don't be silly, you know I can't…'

'Then you'll just have to get wet where you are.'

He pushed himself off. The boat rocked, violently, from side to side.

'Tom Osborne, I'll have you.'

He turned on his back and kicked away.

'Please do, Jessica Brown, be my guest, any time.'

Jess stood up. She sat down in the centre of the boat, where Tom had been sitting, and grabbed the oars.

'Jess, what are you doing…'

She pulled, swiftly and strongly, away from Tom towards the shore.

'What do you think I'm doing? I'm rowing. Like my father taught me…'

He was no longer grinning. He wasn't even smiling.

'You can't…'

Another stroke. And another.

'I can and I will. And nobody, least of all you, Tom Osborne, is going to stop me.'

He was swimming towards her, trying to catch up, but the stronger he swam the stronger she pulled. A crowd of people, mostly young, many in uniform, cheered as she pulled up against the pontoon. She tied up the boat. She picked up Tom's shoes and clothes, hitched up her skirt, stepped up onto the wooden decking and walked, without looking back, down the pontoon towards the promenade which ran around the edge of the lake.

'Jess, please stop.'

She could hear his feet slapping down behind her on the decking.

'I'm sorry, what I said, Jess…'

'Tom, Tom Osborne, is that you?'

A thinner version of the Major was standing staring at them.

'It is you, isn't it, Tom, your parents said you were home on leave.'

A tiny, grey-haired woman, carrying a parasol, her pale face flushed pink, peered out from behind him.

Tom grabbed his clothes. 'Baking hot day – thought I'd go for a swim.' He pulled on his trousers and dragged on his shirt, 'Not much chance of that on the front…bit muddy.'

He shoved his feet into his shoes, pushed his hair off his forehead and stepped forward. The two men shook hands. Tom turned towards Jess.

'Mr and Mrs Hamilton, may I introduce you to Miss Emily Carrington. Mr and Mrs Hamilton are very old friends of my parents.'

'Absolutely charming.'

Mr Hamilton took off his hat and bowed. His wife bobbed her head.

'My dear, it's such a pleasure to meet you.'

She recognised them. The husband had ignored her when he blustered through the front door of Eaton Villa. But his wife had been polite, had even smiled, even insisted on looking her in the eye and said thank you, properly, when Jess had taken her coat.

'Emily is the sister of Mathew Carrington, a brother officer. I promised Mathew I would drop in to see her when I was home on leave.'

Mrs Hamilton plucked at her sleeve.

'Now, both of you, you must join us…'

Standing there, silent, blushing demurely, she could easily be mistaken for the perfect young lady. But her secret would be out as soon as she opened her mouth.

'I'm so sorry, Mrs Hamilton, maybe another time. I promised Emily's mother that I would get her home before six o'clock. If we don't go now we'll be late and I'll never be allowed to see her again.'

The Hamiltons went in one direction. Tom and Jess in another. They parted outside the main entrance to the gardens. Tom would go back in a cab. She would go back on the bus.

Hat and dress off, uniform on, the clocks were just starting to chime six o'clock when she walked into the drawing room.

'Jess, how was your friend, the one from Sussex, the one you were having tea with...'

She bobbed a curtsey.

'Very well, ma'am.'

'And where did you go? You look as though you caught the sun...'

'Marble Arch, ma'am, the Lyons Cornerhouse...'

'How nice, you may go, dinner at eight.'

She bobbed another curtsey and headed for the door.

'Tom, we had a telephone call, from the Hamiltons, just before you got back...'

Jess walked fast, eyes down, out of the drawing room into the hallway.

'They said they met you in Kensington Gardens, something about you going swimming, and a girl...'

Had their secret been discovered?

'Yes, Father, Emily Carrington, sister of Mathew Carrington. A fellow officer, educated at Eton.'

A very good family – even if they didn't exist.

'And this Emily, will you be seeing her again?'

'I very much hope so, Mother. Very often and very frequently.'

Jess stuffed her apron into her mouth. She was halfway down the stairs to the kitchen when the phone rang. Who else had seen them? Still laughing, she stumbled back up the stairs. A deep breath in, a deep breath out, one, two, three and she picked up the receiver.

'The Osborne residence.'

THIRTY-TWO

LYING THERE, SIDE BY side, skin to skin, on top of his narrow bed, she had felt no guilt, none at all, not the first morning, nor any of the days and nights that followed. But tonight, the hours snatched between midnight, when she had finished her work, and five o'clock when she had to get up, get dressed and go down to get the house ready for the family, would be their last time together. Lieutenant Thomas Osborne had been called back to France.

'The scent of your skin? What is it?'

She felt the touch of his lips on the back of her neck.

'Honeysuckle and roses. Spring in an English garden.'

She wanted the clocks to slow down, for time to stand still so the two of them could remain, hidden away, together forever. But the minutes and seconds had ticked away ever faster. How was she going to stay on her own, there in the house, washing and cooking, cleaning and sweeping, pretending that nothing had happened, keeping their happiness a secret, not knowing where he was, whether he was alive or dead, whether she would ever see him again?

'You'll write?'

'That may be difficult.'

Out of the window, way up high, a plane ducked and dived in and out of the searchlights.

'My parents must never find out about us. It would never be allowed. They'd send you away.'

'But it's always me who picks up the post in the hall. Your parents never do it.'

'But what if you're ill? They'd recognise my handwriting.'

'I could get a job in a factory, making munitions. The Woolwich Arsenal would take me. I could lie about my age. It's good money. And there are hostels for–'

'No, Jess. It's dirty, dangerous work. Women are injured and killed all the time and not just a few. You know that, you read the papers, hear it talked about on the streets. Please, stay here, where I know you'll be safe, where I know I'll be able to find you. My parents will look after you. They are decent people.'

'You could send the letters to Ellie next-door. She could pass them on to me?'

He shook his head.

'No, Jess. We can't take the risk.'

He was right. But not ever to hear from him, not ever to get a letter, was too much to bear.

'What about pretending to be someone else?'

'Swap ink for pencil and forget to cross my 't's?'

He slid a finger down her nose.

'I could. It might work. But it would be easier, and safer, if you wrote to me. I'll give you money for stamps, clothes, anything you need. A letter would be something to look forward to.'

He pressed his body up against hers.

'One in the morning…'

He nuzzled his face up against her cheek.

'One in the afternoon…'

She rolled over, laughing, onto her back.

'And one in the evening?'

He pulled a box out from underneath the pillow.

'I have something for you.'

He slipped off the lid. Inside, lying on a tiny, purple velvet cushion was a heart-shaped locket on a chain. He fastened it around her neck.

'Promise me that you will always wear it. Then wherever you are, and wherever you go, we will always be together.'

She slid out of his bed and stood there, naked, looking down at this man she loved, nursing the feeling of his body inside her. He opened his eyes and seeing her there pulled her down to lie beside him. They lay there, two joined into one, until the clocks chimed five.

As the last stroke echoed up through the house, she pulled herself out of his arms. She slipped from his bed and crept from his room, along the corridor, through the door and up the narrow flight of stairs into the attic. She poured water out of the jug into the bowl and, picking up a cloth, washed herself clean of his touch and smell.

THIRTY-THREE

SHE SLEEPWALKED, HER BODY brushing the carpets and shaking out the mats, drawing up the blinds, pulling back the curtains and opening the windows, while her head and her heart remained curled up, beside her lover, in his bed, at the top of the house.

She wanted desperately, but at the same time dreaded even more desperately, to find herself alone with him. And now here he was – but he wasn't alone. Dressed in a khaki tunic and breeches, his revolver tucked into the holster at his waist, he was sitting at the table in the dining room with his mother and father.

'It says here that Germany is within six months of collapse.' The Major closed his newspaper.

'One more push and the war will be over. Good news, eh?' The Major's wife dabbed at her mouth with a napkin.

'Six months? You'll be home in time for Christmas, Tom.'

She'd heard it said before, the war would be over by Christmas, when the man and the soldiers came to their village to take the boys away. That was three years ago.

'We'll have a holly wreath on the front door…'

Jess could see it, the hope on her face, the need to know that when the war was over everything would be the same as it had been before. But how could it be? When the war started, Jess had had a father, a mother and a baby brother. Now she had no one. And the Major's wife had had three sons. Now she had only one.

'And a big tree in the hallway…'

Jess read the papers, down in the kitchen, when the Major had finished with them, and it was easy to see that the casualty numbers were going up, not down. There were pages and pages of them. And the highest casualty figures were in the ranks of the junior officers.

'If Sir Douglas Haig gets his way, mother, I doubt very much if you'll have any sons at all by the time it gets to Christmas.'

This wasn't her Tom talking. It was another Tom, thin-lipped and straight-backed, sitting at the table.

'I'm sorry, Jess.'

He was looking up at her.

'I know you had to queue for hours.'

The Major and his wife had eaten their breakfast but their son's remained untouched. She bobbed her head.

'Sir.'

She leant across to remove his plate. His eyes on her face, the warmth of his breath on her cheek, she could feel him but she couldn't look. And she couldn't touch. She didn't dare. His parents would see and she would be thrown out of the house onto the street.

The Major's wife rose from the table.

'If you would excuse me.'

Tom and his father stood.

'Jess, clear breakfast and then come up. We need to talk about today's shopping list.'

Today just for once, the opening and the stripping, the airing and the clearing, and the brushing and the sweeping, and the Major's wife and her shopping list, they could all wait. She sat down at the kitchen table and she ate, down to the last crumb, the egg and bacon on toast that Tom had left for her on his plate. Would they, one day in the future, be able to sit down in the same room, at the same table, to eat a meal together?

She pushed the thought away. Just get through today. That would be difficult enough. Tomorrow, the future, whatever it held, would have to wait.

She climbed back up the stairs to the ground floor. The door leading into the living room was closed. Eavesdropping on your master and mistress' conversations was something Ellie had insisted she should learn how to do. Particularly when the conversations were taking place behind closed doors – because that was when they were talking about you. She leant her ear up against the door. She could hear nothing. The Major and his son were doing their talking quietly.

She went up the stairs to the first floor and knocked on the bedroom door.

'Enter.'

The Major's wife was sitting, a notebook open on her lap and pen in hand, beside the window. There was a real chance if she was sent out shopping, and had to queue at more than one shop, that she wouldn't get back until after Tom had left. Perhaps it would be better that way. Having to remain silent, with her eyes down, as he walked past her and out of the door was going to be more than she could bear.

'We haven't talked about your mother.'

Jess stiffened.

'Tom tells me that she had a cold and it went to her chest…'

They'd agreed a plan. Her mother had died from pneumonia. Suicide, however desperate the situation, would be regarded by the Major and his wife as a sign of weakness, unreliability, even insanity.

'Yes, ma'am.'

And if the mother was insane then it was more than likely that her daughter would be too.

'She went quickly and with no pain. A good life…'

The Major's wife closed her notebook.

'And a good death.'

145

She put down her pen.

'There's no shopping for you to do today. The Major and I have eaten more than enough. We will make do with whatever is left in the larder...'

Jess curtseyed.

'Yes, ma'am.'

'You may go.'

She turned towards the door.

'Tom has also asked whether it would be possible for us to pay you for the work you do here.'

Ellie was on ten pounds a year but Jess couldn't expect that. The house next-door was Ellie's third job; she was far more experienced.

'The Major and I have discussed it and we feel that it would be best if we keep to the agreement we made with your mother. You've been here less than three months. And you came here knowing nothing. And it costs us money to feed and clothe you.'

One pound, two pounds, even just ten shillings, would make all the difference.

'When you've been here a year and have proved that you are capable of performing all the duties that are expected of you, without instruction, then we will reconsider the situation.'

She was worth nothing, not a pound, not a shilling, not a single penny.

'But you will always have a home here. For however long you want to stay.'

She curtseyed.

'Thank you, ma'am.'

'You may go.'

She wanted to find Tom, to thank him for what he had tried to do, but wherever he was and wherever she went either the Major or his wife, or both of them, were always with him.

And now, finally, three hours later but just seconds before

he was due to leave, here they were, alone together in the dining room. She tightly buttoned up in her maid's uniform. He tightly buttoned up in his officer's uniform.

'You'll wait for me.'

He stepped towards her.

'Promise you'll wait for me.'

The glass in the windows shook.

'I will come back.'

The ground under their feet trembled. The war had taken her father and now it was going to take her lover. The dogs were streaming down the hill towards the fox sitting, hunched, waiting for death, in the ditch – and there was nothing she could do to stop them.

'Tell me that you love me, Jess. Tell me that you love me...'

She stepped towards him.

'I–'

'Tom?'

The Major's wife was standing in the doorway.

'Your father's found a cab.'

Jess turned towards the dining table.

'It's waiting outside. Hurry now, you mustn't be late for your train.'

And now the clocks were striking mid-day. He was walking along the hallway and she was standing there, eyes down, holding the front door open, his locket round her neck burning into her flesh. He was kissing his mother's cheek and shaking his father's hand. He was turning to look at her and nodding the nod that a son of the house would give to the maid-of-all-work. He was putting on his cap and she was curtseying and he was walking out of the house, down the steps, and across the pavement to where his cab was waiting.

And her heart and her soul were both screaming, 'Don't go, or if you have to go, then take me with you.'

THIRTY-FOUR

THE BUS SLOWED. THE doors opened and closed and she was left, standing alone in the rain, in a main road lined with four-storey late-Victorian houses. She turned and headed back in the direction the bus had come from. Grand Avenue, Acacia Grove, Victoria Road, the names which had once meant everything, a good education and a good family, a house in a street you and your wife could be proud of, now meant peeling windowsills, kicked in front doors and piles of rotting rubbish.

The houses gave way to a parade of shops: a carpet supplier, an electrician, a hairdresser, a butcher and a baker, all boarded up. Squeezed between the electrician and the hairdresser was a squat, red brick building. There was no sign or notice board but it looked like some sort of community hall. The doors were open and propped up outside on the pavement was a blackboard advertising soup and a sandwich for 50p.

'Jane, dear, why don't you bring that heater over? This poor girl is blue with cold.'

The woman's hair was grey, her back was stooped and her hands were crooked but her eyes sparkled like a child's.

'Why don't you sit yourself down, dear?'

She was pushed, very gently, into a chair.

'There's nothing like tomato soup on a chilly day. And, for the sandwich, we've got either ham or cheese?'

There was a gust of warm air against her leg.

'There you go, now. That should do it. And why don't you take your coat off and put it over the back. You and it will dry faster. And, Jane, dear, couldn't she have a bit of both, ham and cheese?'

'Yes, Joan, I'm sure we can manage that.'

Sam looked from right to left and then from left to right. She blinked and blinked again. Jane and Joan were identical. They were even wearing the same checked skirt, white blouse and blue cardigan. And they had the same dancing eyes.

Jane disappeared through a door.

'That's better. Now, dear, what's your name?'

Joan pulled up a chair.

'Sam. Sam Foster.'

'We haven't seen you here before…'

Rows of wooden chairs stretched through to a platform at the front of the hall. Vases of white lilies stood either side of a podium. "God is Love. God is Light" was written in large gold letters on the wall behind it. She'd only been in a church once and that was for her grandmother's funeral. She stood up.

'I think perhaps…'

Joan grabbed hold of her hand. 'There's a bed, no, several beds, and lots of machines, in a place that's high up, that has no windows…'

Could it be the intensive care unit? If it was, how did she know?

Sam sat back down. Joan patted her hand.

'That's better.'

The door opened. Jane walked out of the kitchen carrying a tray.

'Eat up, dear, you don't want it to get cold.'

She now had a twin sitting either side of her.

'Jane, dear, did you remember?'

'Yes, Joan, dear, in its usual place in the cupboard over the top of the fridge.'

The sandwich was piled high with ham and cheese.

'So what's happened, Sam? Why aren't you at school?'

Chutney oozed out between the slices of bread.

'My dad's in hospital…'

The twins nodded.

'He's got a haemorrhage, in his head, it happened yesterday…'

Joan leant forward in her chair.

'And what do the doctors say, dear?'

Joan had seen the hospital. What else might she be able to see?

'He will be all right, won't he?'

Joan shook her head.

'I'm sorry, my dear, but we can't say what you want us to say because we simply don't know and to lie would be wrong.'

She reached out and took Sam's hand.

'But whatever happens, however bad it gets, you must never give up. Just ask for help and it will come. Because help is always near…'

She needed help now.

'I'm seeing things but I'm not just seeing them, it's like I'm there, like I'm somebody else, walking down the street, wearing their clothes…'

Joan nodded.

'And when I woke up in my room, yesterday, and this morning, when I was with Dad, at the hospital…'

Joan smiled.

'Being different, seeing things, hearing things, going to places other people can't, is a gift – a very special one. But it isn't easy. Five hundred years ago, they would have called you a witch or a heretic. You would have been tortured, stoned, even burnt at the stake.'

Joan leant back in her chair.

'There's a girl. She's waiting for you. You'll recognise her when you see her.'

She closed her eyes.

'Come now, Sam, it's time for you go.'

She followed Jane towards the door.

'Is she… all right?'

Joan's eyes were still tightly closed.

'A cup of strong, hot tea and a biscuit always works wonders.'

Sam threw her rucksack over her shoulder.

'Thank you for the sandwich, and the soup. They were both lovely.'

She pulled out her purse.

'I need to pay you.'

'No. No. That won't be necessary.'

'But it said on the–'

'When Joan was five years old, she was outside in the garden and, suddenly, there was her favourite uncle, Jack. Nobody had said that he was coming for a visit but there was nothing else odd about it. He was just her usual Uncle Jack. She ran inside to tell our mother and the phone went. It was her Aunt Alice. Uncle Jack was dead. He had died that morning from a heart attack.'

Joan glanced over Sam's shoulder.

Sam turned to look. The street was empty.

THIRTY-FIVE

SHE TWISTED THE KEY in the lock. The door opened and got stuck. She kicked it.

If being "different" meant spending the afternoon with two spooky old ladies, in some weird church in the middle of nowhere, then whoever or whatever it was who was trying to suck her up into their life could stick it. If it dared to come back, she wouldn't allow it in. She would order it to go away.

'I'm home.'

She threw her rucksack down, took off her jacket and hung it, in its usual place, next to her father's coat. She buried her nose in the sleeve. He was there. It was him; the father who used to pick her up when she was very little, swing her up and over his shoulders, so she could sit there, the queen in her very own castle, looking out at her kingdom, the rivers, the fields and the hills, rolling away as far as she could see.

'I'm in the kitchen.'

Her mother peered at Sam over her glasses.

'I didn't expect you until after the fireworks.'

Sam slumped down at the table.

'Heard anything?'

'I called an hour ago. No change. How was school?'

'OK.'

She shouldn't have run away. She should have stayed with Katie, Lou and Shelly and she should have gone to the fireworks. This time last year, the four of them, just girls, there had been no boys, had sat on the beach, stuffing themselves with fish and chips, oohing and ahhing at the rockets exploding up into the sky. It wasn't their fault they didn't understand. How could they? If it had been Katie's father in hospital then she, Sam, would have behaved in exactly the same way.

Her mother's mobile rang.

'Hello, Rachel Foster speaking.'

It was a man.

'Right, yes. How long do you think it will take? Yes, I understand.'

Her mother was doing the listening rather than the talking.

'Thank you. Yes, we're fine. Thank you for letting us know. Yes, I'll be here all evening.'

She put the phone down.

'That was Mac.'

It wasn't good news. She knew that already, without her mother having to tell her.

'There's too much pressure on the brain so they're going to have to drill a hole and suck off some blood. It's a routine procedure. They'll call when it's over. Shouldn't take more than one, maybe two, hours...'

Her mother closed her laptop.

'Do you want something to eat? There's the chicken casserole, the one we were supposed to have yesterday...'

Her mother upstairs in the bedroom crying, Sam downstairs in the kitchen getting drunk, just thinking about it made her to want to creep upstairs and crawl under her duvet.

'Thank you for taking it out of the oven...'

Had she?

'Casseroles are always better the next day...'

If she had, and she must have done, if that's what her mother said, she had no memory of doing so.

'No, thanks, I'm not hungry. Maybe later...'

Her mother picked up her mobile.

'I'll let you know if I hear anything...'

She unlocked the door that led out onto the small balcony. A jumble of rooftops, a straggle of grass, a strip of shingle and there was the sea. Tonight it was calm. But when the wind and rain howled in off the Channel, standing out there, on the balcony, was like being the captain on the bridge of a ship.

And that would be where her father could always find her when the weather was rough. He would come up to her room and they would go outside onto the balcony. Together, side by side, they would battle the towering waves that threatened to suck the two of them down into the depths of the deep, dark ocean. But her father wasn't standing beside her – she would be doing the battling alone.

There was a long, drawn-out sigh, followed by the tearing of the air. The surrounding darkness was split by a flash of white light as a rocket shot into the sky. She expected to see the lights on the promenade twinkling off into the distance, the wings of the angel statue silhouetted against the moonlit sky, the cliffs standing sentinel at either end of the town. But what she expected no longer existed.

Stretching out ahead was a vast wasteland; a filthy, oozing sea of mud studded with the blackened stumps of lifeless trees. Craters, filled with slimy water, touched and overlapped all the way to the horizon. Beaten down into this mess were bits of equipment, helmets, rifles, coils of barbed wire, even a military tank.

A gold ring, embedded in a piece of rock, lay beside her feet. She looked more closely. The piece of rock wasn't rock but a human finger. As she looked even more closely, the finger connected itself to a hand, a hand attached itself to an arm, a head stuck itself onto a neck, the neck onto a back with two shoulders. The bones jerked and a rat, as big as a cat, tore itself out of the ribcage of a man who used to be somebody's husband.

The sea of mud wasn't that at all. It was a sea of blood

and bones. There were arms, legs, heads and hands, some still wearing clothes, some still with eyes and hair, layer upon layer of them. And the blood and the bones weren't all dead. Some were still alive and still suffering. Their cries rose up all around her.

A head rose up. A pair of blue eyes blinked. And blinked again.

'Jess...'

It reached a hand out towards her.

'Jess...'

THIRTY-SIX

SHE PUSHED OPEN THE first set of double doors.

'I am not Jess. And I don't want to be. Not now. Not ever.'

And then the second.

'My mother is Rachel Foster.'

She marched up to the nursing station.

'My father is Michael Foster.'

'And you're Samantha Foster, you live at 7 Seaview Road and your mother called an hour ago...'

Mac swivelled round in his chair. He wasn't smiling.

'She said you went up to your room and the next thing you were running out of the house like a bat out of hell. You didn't say where you were going, what you were doing, nothing...'

She'd had to get away, run away as far as she could, as fast as she could.

'I want to see Dad...'

Mac stood up.

'He's still in theatre. But he should be back –'

The telephone on the desk buzzed.

'Hello, County Hospital, Intensive Care Unit. Yes, speaking.'

Mac smiled at her.

'We were just going to ring you. Yes, Sam's here, just arrived, safe and sound. I'll pass you over...'

She took the phone.

'Hello, Mum. Yes, I'm fine. I'm sorry...'

Another phone on the desk started buzzing. A nurse, one she hadn't seen before, reached over to answer it.

'I wanted to be with Dad. No, he's not here. He's still in theatre. Yes, that's what Mac said...'

She handed the phone back.

'Mum wants to talk to you.'

'Hello, Mrs Foster. No, there's nothing to worry about. Like I said, it's just a routine procedure, one they do every day. Yes, I'll ring you as soon as your husband arrives back on the ward...'

It had started, these slips into another life, this Jess' life, at the fair on the ghost train, the same evening she'd come home to find her mother telling her father to pack his bags and not come back. Maybe if he got well, if he came home, the slips would end.

'Yes, she's fine. No problem at all. Yes. We'll see you later.'

He put the phone down.

'You can stay here, wait for your father to come back and your mother to come and collect you, on one condition...'

She followed Mac down the corridor, between the cubicles, to the end of the ward. Her father's cubicle was empty but lying on the bed, in the opposite cubicle, was an elderly man.

'This is Terry. Terry may or may not be his name but it's better than nothing. He was found lying unconscious out on the street and was brought in by ambulance yesterday morning. No ID, no papers, no wallet, no nothing, just the clothes he was wearing and 'Terry' written inside the neck of his shirt. He'd had a heart attack but he's stable now, doing just fine. He's up here because we're waiting for a bed to become free downstairs and then he'll be transferred.'

The old man's eyes were closed and he was snoring.

'So what's the condition?'

'We're hoping, if he knows that someone's here, if he can hear someone talking to him, that he'll regain consciousness.

157

He's got no one, no friends, no family, nobody, so just give it a go, talk to him, just say whatever comes into your head. I'll come back later to see how you're getting on.'

Mac walked off and she was left, standing there alone, in the cubicle. There was just one chair and it was at the far end of the bed. She moved it closer to the old man and sat down.

'Hello, Terry. My name's Sam.'

She stared down at the grey face thick with stubble.

'My dad's here, in the same ward as you…'

The old man snored on.

'…In the cubicle opposite. He's not here now, he's downstairs with the doctors. They're drilling a hole in his head…'

She shouldn't be going on about her father. But what else was there to talk about? She didn't know anything about him. Bleep. Bleep. Bleep. Heartbeat steady. Breathing regular.

Where he lived? Who were his friends? Whether he had any family? Bleep. Bleep. Bleep. And, even if she did think of something to say, did they really believe that he would be able to hear her?

The bleep of the monitor, hooked up beside the bed, caught for a moment and then continued on as before.

And if he could hear her, would talking to him make any difference?

The bleep stopped and then re-started. But it was no longer a bleep – it was a loud, angry scream. And the old man who had been locked away in his coma was sitting upright, straight as a rod, with his arms outstretched, his eyes staring and his mouth opening and closing as if trying to say something.

THIRTY-SEVEN

THE CRASH TEAM RUNNING down the ward pushing a red trolley laden with equipment, the doctor shouting instructions, the nurses filling syringes and inserting tubes, the old man's body convulsing as the electricity shot through it; the hospital was the last place she wanted to be.

She banged the button to the side of the lift. Nothing. She banged the button again. And still nothing. At the far end of the corridor there was an emergency exit sign and below it a door. She ran, twisting and turning, down the stairs, past department after department, Obstetrics, Paediatric, Orthopaedic, Vascular, Cardiology...

Some more stairs, a set of doors, turn right, down a corridor and she was in the hospital's main reception.

'Excuse me...'

A policewoman was walking towards her.

'What are you doing here? '

A policeman joined her.

'I'm sorry...'

Why were they questioning her?

'It's late, shouldn't you be at home?'

She'd done nothing wrong.

'I'm visiting my father. He's a patient here.'

'What's your name?'

The policewoman was doing the talking, the policeman the looking up and down.

'Sam. Sam Foster.'

The policeman was turning away. He was talking on his radio.

'Which ward is your father on, Sam?'

The policeman was checking up on her.

'Intensive care.'

The policewoman's face softened.

'What happened?'

'It was a car accident. A girl ran out in front of him. He braked but his seatbelt jammed and he hit his head...'

'When was he admitted?'

'Yesterday morning, early, he was on his way to work...'

The policewoman glanced over to her colleague. He shook his head.

'Where are you off to now?'

'Home.'

She couldn't think of anything else to say.

'OK, Sam. I'm sorry to have bothered you.'

The policewoman smiled.

'I hope your dad pulls through.'

A bus was drawing up at the stop outside. She couldn't see what number it was but it would be warm and dry and none of her fellow passengers would know or care who she was, what she was doing or where she was going.

The bus drove on down the main road. Valley Cross, North Way, Sutton Avenue, she didn't recognise any of the names. Past a clock tower encrusted with pigeons, a row of shops selling nothing that anyone would need or want or even like – zebra-skin rugs, presumably fake, and posters of crushed Coco Cola cans – and a concrete lump of building which looked like a prison but which turned out, seconds later, when they drove past a noticeboard, to be a town hall.

A girl was waiting at a pedestrian crossing. The traffic lights went from amber to red. The bus slowed and stopped. But the girl didn't move. She just stood there, at the side of the road, staring up at Sam sitting in the bus. The lights changed to green and the bus moved forward. But still the girl stood there.

You'll recognise her when you see her.

Sam jumped out of her seat.

'Stop, please, stop.'

The driver ignored her.

'Please stop the bus. I need to get off...'

It was the girl she'd seen that morning, standing on the opposite side of the road to the house.

'Next stop's Beacon Road.'

'Please, it's an emergency...'

'That's what they all say.'

The bus-driver slammed his foot down hard on the accelerator. Sam slammed her hand down even harder on the buzzer by the doors. Maybe the two old ladies in the church weren't mad.

'Are you deaf or dumb or something?'

She put her hand back on the buzzer. She pushed it once. She pushed it twice. Maybe the girl standing at the crossing was, in some way Sam couldn't yet understand, waiting for her. She pushed it again and again. The bus screeched to a halt. The doors slammed open.

Sam ran back up the street and then left onto the main road. The pedestrian crossing was immediately ahead but there was no sign of the girl. But she hadn't had time to go far. Sam ran down to the next corner. She looked left, Firfield Way, nothing. She ran, straight ahead, along the main road. She looked down a second street, Hazel Avenue, and then a third, Tudor Close.

And there she was. Sam could just see her, walking up a garden path, halfway down the road. Sam ran down the terrace. She stopped outside the house. Standing there, looking out of the ground floor bay window was the girl. And she was smiling.

Sam didn't think twice, she pushed open the gate, walked up the path and rang the bell. There was no answer. She rang it again. The door opened.

'Hello?'

It was a girl.

'Long coat, lace-up boots, brown hair…'

But this one had short reddish-blonde hair and was wearing leggings.

'You've got the wrong–'

'But I saw her, just now, looking out of the window. She walked into this house just seconds ago…'

'No, I'm sorry, you've made a mistake.'

The girl had stood there, looking out of the window, smiling, inviting Sam in. So why was this girl, the one standing here at the front door, lying?

THIRTY-EIGHT

September 1917

'I'VE BEEN WAITING FOR hours...'

They had arranged to meet at their usual place, the corner of Wakehurst Street and Northcote Avenue, at ten o'clock sharp. It was now eleven.

'Ellie, I tried to get away but she wouldn't make up her mind about anything. Did she want potatoes, didn't she want potatoes. Did she want meat, didn't she want meat, and if she did want meat, did she want beef or pork. I wanted to tell her that she would be lucky if she got cat. And then she got onto bread. Did we need some, didn't we need some, and I just wanted to say if you don't get a move on, you silly old bag, there won't be any bread. But I didn't.'

She couldn't. If she had she would have been out of a job.

They linked arms and walked together, baskets swinging, past the old man playing the barrel organ with a monkey, dressed in a moth-holed woollen suit, spitting and gibbering on his shoulder.

A crowd had gathered outside the butcher. Men, women and children stood in a circle, laughing and jeering at two women shouting abuse at each other. The younger woman grabbed the older woman's hair. The older woman scratched her nails down the younger woman's face. The younger woman kicked. The older woman kicked back. A little boy began to cry.

'Come on now...'

Two men walked out of the crowd. They pulled the two women apart.

'That's enough.'

Walking towards them, down the street, was a young soldier.

'Look at him, that's what I call a man. He's got everything a woman needs or wants…'

'Ellie, that's an awful thing to say.'

'Awful? What's awful about it? It's the truth. Just look at that one over there…'

A young woman was pushing a wheelchair along the pavement on the opposite side of the street. Propped up in the chair was a man. Or what was left of a man. He was hunched over, as if his spine had been snapped in two, and his head was lolling on his chest. He had just one arm and one leg.

'Look at that poor bastard. Whatever they pay him it won't be enough. And what sort of life is she going to have?'

'Ellie…'

'Pushing that thing around for the rest of her–'

'Please, Ellie…'

The tears were coming.

'I mean just look at him. It's not right…'

She couldn't stop them.

'I'm going to have… a baby…'

It was out.

'A baby?'

Ellie leaned forward. She lowered her voice.

'Are you sure?'

'Yes, yes, of course I'm sure.'

'But, Jess, you might have made a mistake. Got the dates wrong? What about your monthly…'

She'd crossed the days off, one by one. And then the weeks, one by one.

'Nothing for two months.'

'Two months? Why didn't you tell me? Why didn't you say something?'

And now Ellie was whispering.

'Who is he?'

Ellie was like a sister, even a mother, to Jess, all rolled into one. She wouldn't have survived the first few weeks in London without her. And it would have seemed the most natural thing in the world to tell her about Tom. But she had kept her promise.

'It's not that one, him with the earring, who delivers the coal, because, Jess, I've got to tell you now—'

'It's Tom. Tom's the father.'

Ellie froze.

'Tom? That Tom?'

'Yes, that Tom.'

Ellie's eyes widened.

'The bastard, taking advantage of you, right there in his own home, it's disgusting, an innocent girl like you…'

Ellie's hands were clamped on her hips, her head was thrust forward and her eyes were bulging.

'You're fifteen, too young to get married, definitely too young to be pregnant and you've got no home and no parents…'

Jess started to laugh.

'What's so funny? Because, from where I'm standing, things don't look so good.'

'What you just said, about Tom taking advantage of me? That's what you told me to do, "Get yourself in there, get yourself in the family way and then you'll be looked after." Remember?'

'And that's what you did?'

'Come on, Ellie, I'm not that stupid. I may be a maid-of-all-work but I know what's right and I know what's wrong and I've still got some pride.'

Ellie scowled.

'And I suppose the next thing you're going to tell me is that you love him?'

'Yes, yes, I do. And he loves me.'

Ellie's laugh was loud and harsh.

'That's what they all say. Love? You wouldn't know, Jessica Brown, what love was if it hit you in the face. What happens if he comes home like that one over there, with no arms, no legs and slobbering like a baby? Will you still love him when he doesn't know who you are, when you have to wash him and wipe him and feed him his soup? Will you? Because, Jess, that's what love is, really is, not this silly little dream, all hearts and flowers and wedding bells and sweet little babies you're carrying around inside your head.'

The wheelchair was sitting outside a shop. The woman was nowhere to be seen but the man was still there, propped up, his head lolling.

'And what if he doesn't come home at all? What if he gets blown to pieces on some battlefield?'

Jess had never seen Ellie cry, not ever, however long the day had been, however tired she was.

'Did you think about that when the two of you were banging away at each other...'

And now tears were streaming down her face.

'Ellie, what's the matter?'

Jess put her arms round her.

'Tell me, what's the matter?'

Ellie pushed her away.

'I didn't want you to know...'

She pulled a handkerchief out of her sleeve.

'I was engaged, a year ago, I had a fiancé, Oliver, he wrote me a letter to say he was coming home on leave and he wanted me to get the church sorted so we could get married.'

Jess waited while Ellie snuffled into her handkerchief.

'He was due back Wednesday. I waited and waited and then the telephone rang, in the afternoon. My mistress called me and I was so excited, I thought it was him. But it wasn't...'

Ellie blew her nose.

'It was his father. Ollie's ship had been torpedoed, the one bringing him back home from France…'

She pushed the handkerchief up her sleeve. She picked up her shopping basket.

'Danger and delight, Jessica Brown,' she hooked her arm inside Jess', 'grow on one stalk.'

THIRTY-NINE

'Are you sure?'

Jess sighed.

'Ellie, I can't do anything else. If he loves me, he'll write to his parents, tell them that I'm expecting, and then they'll have to look after me.'

'But what if–'

'He doesn't love me? Well, then, what will happen will be what always happens when an underage girl like me, with no family and no home, gets herself pregnant. I'll be kicked out onto the streets, and I'll have nowhere to go except the workhouse. My baby, if it's born alive, and if I don't die having it, will be taken away from me. And I'll spend the rest of my life shut up behind four walls, my head shaved, dressed in nothing but a sack…'

If only half of what she was saying was true. Having to go into a workhouse was not something anyone should joke about. Jess had seen the one in Lewes. Her mother had lowered her eyes and pulled on Jess's hand, rushing her past the imposing grey-stone entranceway. She'd explained that it was a place nobody would choose to go to unless they were really desperate. It was where the poor, the old and the sick ended up if they had no one to look after them. Most of those who entered never left. They ended up dying there.

But the workhouse wasn't just for the old. It was where she would be sent, an unmarried girl expecting a baby.

'He said he loved me. He really did…'

'That's what they all say, just so they can get their sticky fingers inside your knickers…'

'Tom's not like that.'

'They're all like that, every single one of them.'

'Even your Ollie?'

Ellie smiled.

'Even my Ollie.'

On any other night she would have found the letter easy to write. She would just imagine Tom lying there beside her, their heads side by side on the pillow, and she would tell him everything that she had done that day. But after fifty-six letters, eight weeks of writing one letter a day, she was more than aware that she had been writing the same things over and over again.

Telling the man you loved, who was risking his life out in France, who woke up each morning never knowing whether he'd be dead or alive one hour later, that you had got up at five o'clock, swept the floors, shaken the rugs out, scrubbed the front steps, polished the doorknobs, cooked breakfast, made the beds, gone shopping and sorted out the laundry might have been good enough for people like her father and her mother, a farm labourer and his wife, but it wouldn't do for Tom. Not at all. She would have to try harder.

So she'd started to comment on the things she'd read in the papers to make her letters more interesting. And sometimes she made up stories. They were always funny and they always had happy endings. But this letter was different. The story she was about to write was true. And it didn't, as yet, have an ending. And, when it did, she wasn't convinced that it would be a happy one.

'Your father and mother have got me digging up the back garden, the grass and all the lovely flowers, the roses, and everything, so that we can grow vegetables, carrots and onions and potatoes and swede. They will make a lovely soup…'

Ellie yawned.

'Queues at the shops are getting longer – good job there's just the three of us to feed…'

Ellie snorted.

'More like four.'

'Ssh, they'll hear you.'

'No they won't. They're two floors down and the Major snores like a pig. Get a move on, will you.'

'Where was I?'

Ellie rolled her eyes.

'There's talk of the government giving people cards, rationing food, I don't know if it's a good idea. But people need something to eat. There's been rioting, crowds breaking into shops, attacking the shopkeepers but there's nothing to buy. We have been reading in the papers about the fighting at…'

She nudged Ellie.

'How do you spell it?'

Ellie smoothed out the newspaper that Jess had sneaked out from under the Major's chair that evening.

'P …a …s …s …c …h …e …n … 'Jess wrote out the name, letter by letter, 'd …a …e …l …e.'

She had told Ellie, two days ago, when they were out shopping, that she was expecting Tom's baby. It had been an ordinary Thursday in south London, no different from any other, with the Major complaining, as usual, about the dust she hadn't brushed off the carpet and his wife unable to make up her mind about whether they did or didn't need bread.

But on that same day, 20th September, near a village called Passchendaele in Belgium, a village not unlike her own with cottages, some big, some small, clumped together round a church, 21,000 allied soldiers had been killed or wounded at the Battle of Menin Road Bridge. All those boys, all those men; it was impossible to understand, impossible to take in. But it was all too easy, if you just thought of each one, singly; a son, a brother, a husband or a father, a Tom, standing outside his home, surrounded by his family.

'My darling Tom, I hope you're not there but somewhere far away where you are safe. I wear your locket all the time. I never take it off. You are in my heart every minute of every day...'

Ellie jumped up on the bed.

'I'm off. All that stupid lovey-dovey stuff...'

She pulled back the curtains and wriggled out of the window. Jess watched as her friend made her way, step by step, along the narrow ledge that ran along the front of the two houses. The two girls waved to each other and Ellie slid through the window down into her bedroom. Jess closed her own window, drew the curtains and then ran over to the fireplace. She rapped twice on the wall. Two raps came back.

She picked up the pencil.

'I have some news. I hope that you will be pleased. I have missed two monthlies. I didn't tell you after the first one, in case it was a mistake, but now I've missed a second one so I think a baby must be on its way...'

She couldn't avoid it any longer.

'Please don't be angry with me. I know that you asked me not to tell Ellie about us. But I had to tell her about the baby and now she is helping me. We can trust her. She had a fiancé, Oliver, a soldier who was killed, so she understands.'

The gold locket he'd given her so that they would always be together; his plea, tell me that you love me, standing there in his uniform holding her in his arms; his mother walking down the hallway, the clock striking twelve; asking her to wait for him, promising her that he would come back...

'So please write to me but send the letter to Ellie next-door at Vanbrugh Villa. Address it to Eleanor Baxter and she will give it to me. I will wait here until you tell me what to do. And please don't worry. We are both, mother and baby, doing well.'

She had to find out, for better or worse, one way or another. Everything he'd said, everything he'd done, was it the truth? Or was it a lie?

'Your loving Jess.'

FORTY

October 1917

SHE GAGGED AND GAGGED again but nothing came up: her stomach was empty. She was twelve weeks gone and the sickness was getting worse rather than better. And it wasn't just in the morning but throughout the day. The only food she could eat was dry toast. The only liquid that stayed down was water. She was skin and bone with a bulging ball of a belly which, day by day, if not hour by hour, was getting larger and larger.

It was four weeks since she had written to Tom telling him that she was pregnant. Each morning when she got up, she hoped that this would be the day when she heard something back. When she met up with Ellie later in the morning, she would be standing there, at their usual meeting place, but this time she would be holding a letter in her hand.

Jess would tear open the envelope and read the words that both she and Ellie had been longing to hear; Tom loved her, he was delighted with their news, he was writing to his parents without delay, she shouldn't worry, everything would be fine. But there had been no such letter.

She didn't want to have to confess her pregnancy to his mother and father. They would, more than likely, just throw her out. But if it came from Tom, if he said that he loved her, and wanted them to keep her on and look after her, they would have to take notice.

Had his mother guessed what had happened between them? If she had she gave no clue even when her maid-of-all-work spilt the soup or dropped a plate at the mention of her son's name. When they were alone, going over the daily shopping list, sorting through dirty linen or doing some sewing together, the Major's wife would repeat to her what Tom had said in his letters, where he was, what he was doing. But Tom's last letter home to his parents had arrived over four weeks ago now. Just two days before she'd written her own letter to him. There had been nothing since.

A loud knocking echoed through the house. The chimneys had to be swept every October and this year was to be no exception. Jess had sorted through all the sheets and had selected the ones that were the oldest, greyest and most darned. She would use them to cover the furniture. There would still be dust, lots of it, all over the windows, the shutters, the shelves, everywhere. It would be the grey, sticky sort that was difficult to remove, but at least it would be done for this year. And next year? Next year, where would she be?

What she asked for, when she lay in her bed just before she fell asleep, was that this time next year the war would be over. That she would be safely delivered of a healthy child and that Tom will have arrived back home, neither blind nor deaf, with two arms, two legs and a head, with his brain intact. To ask for anything more, that she should be engaged, even married to him, was just too greedy.

She straightened her cap, smoothed her apron down over the dome of her belly, and ran up the stairs and along the hall to the front door. She opened it. It wasn't the chimney sweep. It was a telegram boy, dressed in his general post office uniform, a bright red pillbox hat perched on the top of his head. She mumbled a thank you, closed the door and stood there in the hall staring down at the envelope. It was addressed to Major and Mrs Osborne. It was either from Tom or about Tom. The families of rank and file soldiers, privates like her own father, got their bad news by letter. The families of officers received their bad news by telegram.

The Major and his wife had gone to call on friends who had just recently lost their own son in the fighting. They wouldn't be back for at least half an hour. And half an hour was too long to stare at this telegram, wondering whether it said that the man she loved, the father of her child, was on his way home on leave, that he was injured or missing – or that he was dead. The envelope was sealed tight but steam would open it. And she had a copper of water boiling on the range.

Ink runs when it gets wet. There had been no rain that morning, or for two days now. If she handed over the envelope, with the names and address all smudged, she couldn't use that as an excuse. The Major and his wife would know, instantly, that someone had tampered with it. And she would be the most likely suspect.

She placed the envelope, face down, onto the back of the *Mrs Beeton's Book of Household Management*. She picked up the book and, with the back of the envelope facing down over the water, held it above the steaming copper. She counted to ten and then lifted the book and the envelope out of the steam and onto the kitchen table. She pulled out a drawer, took out a knife and tried to tease the flap of the envelope open. It was still sealed.

She picked up the book and envelope and, once again, held them over the boiling water. She lifted the book and envelope out of the steam. She put them back down on the table. She picked up the knife and, once again, teased the tip of the blade underneath the flap of the envelope. The tip slid in. The flap lifted.

'Jess, we need to talk about tonight's...'

The Major's wife was standing in the doorway. She and the Major had come home earlier than Jess had expected.

'What are you doing?'

The envelope was lying, clearly open, on the table.

'It came for you, while you were out. It's a—'

175

'I can see what it is.'

The Major's wife came over to the table. She picked up the envelope. She turned it over, checked the address, and then looked up at Jess.

'Have you read it?'

Her voice was as smooth and hard as ice – but also as brittle.

'No.'

The Major's wife pulled out the telegram. She opened it and then read it. Her mouth tightened. She held it out to Jess.

FORTY-ONE

'IT WAS THIS HOUSE. I'm sure of it.'

Sam wedged her foot up against the closing door. There was no point asking for permission. It would only be refused.

'I'm Amy Roberts, I live here, I don't know who you but you can't–'

Sam pushed past the girl, down the hallway, and into the front room. One sofa and two armchairs and, at the far end, in front of a window, impossible to see because the curtains had been drawn, a table with three chairs lined up on either side. A television with armoured vehicles driving along a dusty road on the screen, so probably the news but with the sound turned right down.

A mug, half full of what looked like tea with "No Sugar, I'm Sweet Enough" written on the side. Cards, including one very large, glittery one with "To My Lovely Wife" engraved in gold on the front. A wedding photograph; the woman in a white dress, a veil on her head, carrying a bouquet of white flowers, the man wearing old-fashioned top hat and tails. And next to it a photograph of the same couple, standing side by side; the woman cradling a young baby, presumably the girl who had opened the front door. Behind there was another, smaller photograph, of the same baby beaming up at the camera.

'You can't do this…'

Out of the front room, right down the hallway and into the kitchen. A fridge, one oven, not on, no smell of cooking;

a washing machine in full spin; two apples in a bowl; three plates and one saucepan drying beside the sink; a postcard, blue sea and white beach, pinned to a board, along with lists and leaflets, and more cards. The door out into the garden was locked and there was no sign of a key.

Up the stairs and along the landing. The first bedroom: pink, pink and more pink, with a double bed, presumably the parents', was empty. The second, more of a cupboard than a room, was crammed, every inch of it, with junk: piles of yellowing magazines and newspapers; cardboard boxes overflowing with threadbare towels; a rail crammed with musty smelling clothes; battered holdalls and suitcases, zips broken, handles split, piled up on top of each other in the corner; even a cot, years old, its mattress sagging and stained.

Two more doors: a bathroom and a toilet. Three toothbrushes in three separate mugs, green, yellow and red, towels neatly folded, again nothing. There was just one last door, at the end of the landing. An unmade bed, acid green duvet cover decorated with giant sunflowers, music posters on the walls, clothes, T-shirts and leggings, jumpers and jeans, faded and torn at the knees, scattered all over the floor. A black leather jacket, with a red, blue and silver flash on its sleeve, thrown over the back of a chair.

'Are you on something or what…?'

Charging her way into this house, running from room to room searching for nothing and nobody, poking around where she shouldn't be poking around, this wasn't the same Sam who had gone to the fair with her friends, on the Saturday afternoon, just a couple of days ago.

'I'm sorry. I didn't mean to…'

The front door slammed in her face.

Sam walked back up the path and through the gate. She turned right. Ahead was the main road. Her mother should have received a call from the hospital by now to say that her father was back on the ward and everything was OK. But they would also have told her that Sam was no longer at the hospital; that the old man she'd been sitting with had had a heart attack and she'd run away. Which would mean that her mother would be even more worried now than when Sam first ran out of the house, two or more hours ago.

She turned on her mobile. She would phone and say that she was sorry, that she was fine and that if she caught a bus she would be home in forty-five minutes. There was no need for her mother to drive over to collect her. She punched in the number. The phone rang once, twice, three times. Why wasn't her mother picking up?

The door from the kitchen out into the garden had been locked. It had also been bolted, top and bottom. The girl who'd led her to the house, the only way she could have left, without Sam seeing her, was through that door. Who the girl was, why she was following Sam, why she had led her to the house, were all questions that needed answering. And the person who could provide those answers was Amy. She was the only other person in the house: the only person who could have re-locked and re-bolted that back door.

Sam clicked off the phone, turned and ran back down the road, through the gate, and up the path to the house. The curtains were still open. The lights in the front room still on. She rang the doorbell. No answer. She rang it again. And still no answer.

She flipped open the letterbox. Lying on the floor, in the centre of the hallway, in a pool of blood, was the girl. And the pool of blood was growing larger by the second.

FORTY-TWO

HER LEGS DISSOLVED. SHE slid down onto the ground and dropped her head between her knees. Blood, blood and more blood but fainting wasn't an option; the girl on the other side of the door would die. She pulled her mobile out of her jacket pocket.

'I'm here outside the front door. The girl, Amy, she's inside. No, I don't have a key…'

It was the second time she'd dialled 999 in two days.

'Yes, yes, I understand. Yes, I'll talk to her, try to keep her awake, keep using her name, but you've got to hurry, the bleeding, it's really bad. No, like I said, I can't reach her…'

She knelt up.

'Amy, can you hear me?'

She breathed long and deep.

'You're going to be OK. They're sending an ambulance…'

She pushed open the letterbox.

'There's nothing to worry about…'

She was lying. What had been a pool of blood was now a lake.

'You're going to be fine.'

Fireworks shot up into the sky, a dog howled, a car slowed and then accelerated off down the street.

'They're on their way…'

The girls' eyes flickered.

'It won't be long now…'

And closed.

'Listen to me, Amy…'

She had to keep talking, say anything, however stupid.

'That holiday you went on, the postcard with the blue sea and white beach, the one pinned on the board in the kitchen? You want to go back there, don't you?'

The girl's eyes opened.

'And you can, all of you together, you and your mum and dad…'

No car stopped. No neighbour appeared. Nobody offered to help. Sam crouched there shouting anything she could think of, through the letterbox, to try and stop the girl from closing her eyes.

She was still shouting when the police car pulled up outside the house. The front door was forced open. The girl was loaded into the ambulance.

The accident and emergency waiting room was full, every seat taken, with bonfire night casualties.

'Your address?'

'7 Seaview Road.'

'Your friend's name?'

'Friend?'

'The girl you came in with? In the ambulance?'

'Amy Roberts.'

'Address?'

'Tudor Close.'

'Number?'

A tall figure, dressed in pilot's uniform, gold braid on his sleeves, cap perched at just the right angle on top of his head, was striding towards the entrance doors of the accident and emergency department.

'I'm sorry…'

The automatic doors slid open.

'The house number? In Tudor Close?'

'Twenty-four, I think. I'm not sure…'

The figure disappeared outside.

'No problem. We can check. If you'd like to take a seat I'll get...'

She couldn't wait. She'd done all she could. There was a police car sitting outside the girl's house. When her parents arrived home they would be driven straight to the hospital.

She pushed her way past a family, a little boy his head buried in his father's shoulder, his right hand tightly bound in a wet towel, the mother sobbing into her phone. Behind were two girls, the same age as herself, supporting a third, the side of her face streaked a livid red. The doors slid open. And there he was. Head held high, arms and legs pumping, on his way to somewhere else.

'Dad...'

An ambulance, blue lights flashing, sirens blaring, turned off the main road. It accelerated up the ramp directly towards her father.

'Dad, look out.'

There was no slamming of brakes. No thump of hard metal crunching into soft flesh. The ambulance continued up the ramp. It screeched to a stop outside the accident and emergency department. The driver got out, walked round to the back and threw open first one door, and then the other. An elderly couple looked Sam up and down, shook their heads, muttered something to each other, and continued walking down the ramp towards the main road.

She stood there, trembling, staring at the spot where her father had just been. There had been no slam of brakes, no thump of metal, no screaming or calling out for a doctor, because there had been nothing to scream or call out about. Instead of shattered bone and blood and guts there was empty space. Her father had vanished – if he had ever been there at all.

She ran back into the accident and emergency department,

through the waiting area, and down the corridor to the lift. She punched the button. She stepped inside. The doors closed, the doors opened, people got in, people got out; sixth, seventh, eighth, ninth and, at last, the tenth floor.

'Stand clear... oxygen away...VF... shock.'

A trolley, laden with equipment, stood at the end of her father's bed. She recognised it.

'Asystole. Flat line.'

It was the same trolley the doctors had used to shoot electricity through the old man's body. The old man with the grey face thick with stubble, locked away in his coma, who had suddenly sat upright, straight backed in his bed, his arms outstretched, his eyes staring, his mouth opening and closing as if he was trying to say something. That bed was now empty.

'There's no heartbeat. It's been too long.'

A nurse started to remove an intravenous tube from her father's right arm. A second nurse started to remove an intravenous tube from his left arm. A third nurse unplugged a monitor.

Her father was being tidied up, packed away, like he was nothing more than a head, and a chest, with two arms and two legs which had never felt pain, had never felt anger – had never known love.

She pushed past the trolley, with its plugs and its wires, its paddles and its cables, which had produced the electric shocks that had shot through her father's body, sending him convulsing off the bed. None of which had worked.

'Dad, it's me, Sam.'

She grabbed hold of his hand.

'Please come back.'

Someone was trying to pull her away from the bed.

'Sam, come with me now. Your dad can't hear you...'

It was Mac. Standing next to him was Dr. Brownlow.

'We did everything we could.'

And now Mac was putting his hand on her hand, and he was uncurling it, finger by finger, out of her father's. She kicked out, hitting him hard on the shin. He jumped back. She held on to her father's hand even tighter.

'We love you...'

Her whole body was screaming.

'Please come back...'

She had to make him hear.

'We love you, we love you. Please come back.'

'Sam, stop now, Dad can't hear you...'

She had a special gift. That's what the old lady in the church had said. She could see and hear things other people couldn't see or hear, go to places other people couldn't reach. So where would her father be now? Where would he go, inside his head, if he was in a coma?

She closed her eyes. Sometimes her father would be away for just a couple of days, sometimes a full week, often even longer, but, wherever he was, even if it was on the other side of the world, they had always been able to talk to each other. She had always been able to reach him.

FORTY-THREE

November 1917

'YOU ARE PREGNANT, AREN'T you?'

The needle stabbed into her finger. Blood oozed out onto the sheet.

'The Major thinks I'm just his silly little wife but I'm neither silly, nor am I stupid. Nor am I blind. So are you or are you not pregnant?'

Jess nodded.

'And my son's the father.'

She nodded again.

'And, of course, he loves you.'

Jess raised her eyes.

'Yes, yes, he does, very much.'

For month after month she'd had to walk around the house, her eyes down, her mouth closed, with her swollen belly tightly corseted.

'And you love him.'

Tom had told her that his parents were decent people. And he'd been right. Now, at long last, she could tell the truth.

'Yes, yes, I do.'

Jess put down her sewing.

'Do you think... Tom... do you think he's still alive?'

The telegram had said missing in action. That was over four weeks ago and they had heard nothing since.

'My husband is writing letters and going for meetings with everyone he can. We both believe that Tom will come back home to us.'

The Major's wife turned back to her stitching. Every week, after the linen had been delivered back to Eaton Villa, the Major's wife would check through it, item by item, ticking everything off in her laundry book. Any sheets which were worn thin in the middle had to be cut down the centre and the outside edges sewn together so that the thin bits were on the outside. It took at least a couple of thousand stitches, tiny, almost invisible ones, nothing else would do, to repair one sheet.

'I've always known that one day my son would fall in love and want to get married and have a home of his own. And that's all I have ever wanted, that he should be happy. His father, the Major, however, has always wanted more. Tom, when he comes home, will marry a girl from a good family, with a title and money.'

The Major's wife snipped through her thread.

'A girl like Emily Cunningham.'

The baby kicked out, angrily, against the tightly laced corset she was wearing. It narrowed her waist but only thinly disguised her rounded belly.

'There's no Emily Cunningham, and there's no Matthew Cunningham, never has been. The girl out walking with Tom was me.'

The Major's wife snapped shut the lid of her sewing box.

'And the baby I'm carrying is your son's. Nobody else's. I wrote to Tom four weeks ago telling him I was pregnant, when he received that letter, if he was alive…'

He was. He had to be.

'He would have written to you, asked you to look after–'

'We have received no such letter.'

The Major's wife rose from her chair.

'Please talk to the Major, the child I'm carrying is his grandchild, your grandchild, and always will be, in marriage or out of marriage…'

'And if I do, if I tell him about all the games you've been playing, leading our son on...'

No games had been played and nobody had led anybody on. When the war ended, if Tom came home, maybe he would marry her, maybe he wouldn't. But what she did know was that in the short space of time they'd spent together, something very real had happened between them. And whatever the Major's wife said or did, and however many weeks and months passed, she, Jess, had to try to remember, and hold onto, that truth.

'I know exactly what my husband will say. He will insist on your removal from this house, instantly, with no reference, no money, and with only the clothes on your back. And with your mother dead there will be nowhere for you to go. You'll have no roof over your head and no food on your plate. You will end up walking the streets...'

Five month's pregnant and without a reference would make it impossible for her to find a job.

'If you are with child it cannot and never will be my son's. And you cannot and never will be a member of this family. Now do you still want me to talk to my husband?'

She couldn't take that risk.

'No, ma'am.'

She picked up her sewing.

'So, if you're not pregnant your tiredness and sickness must be due to something else entirely, must they not?'

She lowered her eyes back down to her needlework.

'Yes, ma'am.'

FORTY-FOUR

SHE'D HAD TO WAIT another whole week before the Major and his wife went out in the evening. She needed time – just in case it went wrong.

She untied her apron, the best white for serving dinner, and dropped it down on the chair beside her bed. One, two, three, four, five, six buttons, and she peeled off her black dress. She unlaced and pulled off her corset. She unpinned and then un-tucked the first strip of sheeting. She passed it round and round her body, round and round, gradually easing her breasts out of their prison. She held them in her hands, slowly, slowly, massaging away the pain.

She unpinned and un-tucked the second strip of sheeting. She passed it round her body, again and again, again and again, until it fell to the floor and she was standing there, naked, the gold locket fastened round her neck glinting in the candlelight. She cupped the weight of her swollen belly in her hands, stroking it gently, whispering to the child inside, 'Forgive me, please, forgive me.'

She lowered herself down into the hipbath, sat there in the steaming hot water, stained yellow with mustard powder, waiting, hoping, for the cramps to start. They didn't. She'd tried jumping down off a chair, again and again, but it hadn't worked. Drinking gin wasn't an option. There was none in the house and, even if there was, the Major's wife would have noticed. There was only one more thing she could do. And it was something you only did if you were really desperate. And she was.

Stitch by stitch she unpicked the seam of her corset. The Major's wife had stays made out of whalebone. But she, the maid-of-all-work, had stays made out of beaten steel. They weren't only cheap. They were also very hard and very sharp; when she was kneeling down or bending over she could feel the metal digging into her hips and belly. And something hard and sharp was exactly what she needed. She pulled the stay, inch by inch, out of its seam. It was about as half as wide as her little finger, very thin and completely flat. Both ends were slightly rounded.

Tom knew, from her last letter to him, that she was pregnant. If he was still alive, and he did come home, he would expect to find her with child. Her own mother had lost two babies, one at six weeks, the other three months into pregnancy before being safely delivered of her brother. It wasn't unusual. And that's what she would tell him. That she had lost the baby. And he would believe her. And understand.

She saw him running up the steps, through the front door and into the hallway of the house. He would scoop her up in his arms and hold her so tight that it was impossible to breathe. Then she saw them standing together, side by side, in front of an altar, Tom slipping a gold ring onto her finger.

She was lying in a white bed in a sun-filled room. Tom was standing looking down at her. She held the child up to him. He took their newborn in his arms. Happy, smiling, he cradled it in his arms. It was then that she noticed the little girl, standing at the end of the bed, staring at her. She went back to the church and there was the same little girl, standing between herself and Tom at the altar. And there she was again, standing in the hallway of the house, pulling at Tom's trousers, trying to get his attention. Her lie would follow them everywhere.

But he wasn't coming home. He was missing in action. That's what the telegram had said. And he was missing because no body had been found. And that was because there was no body to find. He had been blown to pieces, his fingers and toes, eyes and ears, just lumps of dead flesh flying through the air.

And the child inside her was nothing more than a lump of flesh. No more. No less. Yes, it was alive, it twisted and kicked, but it didn't feel joy. It didn't know fear. And it didn't feel pain. It didn't matter whether it lived or died. It wouldn't know or care.

She poured water out of the jug into the bowl. She washed and dried the metal stay. Without the child she had a chance. She would work out her time here at Eaton Villa, get the Major and his wife to give her a reference and then she would apply for a better job with decent pay. She would start her life all over again. Years from now, married with a husband and children, all of this would be forgotten.

She spread out an old sheet on the floor, in the narrow space between the bed and the door, and lay down. She hitched her nightdress up above her waist.

'What you trying to do? Kill yourself?'

Ellie jumped down through the open window.

'Because if you are there's no better way of doing it...'

She grabbed the steel from Jess' hand.

'Come here, you silly girl.'

She heaved Jess up from the floor.

'So what's happened, because something must have?'

She pulled her down onto the bed. They lay, side by side, arms wrapped round each other.

'She knows, I told her, but she already knew, she'd already guessed...'

They hugged the blanket around themselves to keep warm.

'So what did she say?'

'It can never be Tom's...'

'So whose is it then? The Archangel bleeding Gabriel's?' Ellie snorted. 'What else did the old bag say?'

'The Major would throw me out if he knew…'

'Listen, Jess, they want you to get rid of it and they'll be dead chuffed if they can get rid of you at the same time. But you mustn't let them. You want to keep this baby, don't you?'

It was easy to say but not so easy to do.

'Tom's dead, he's been blown to pieces, he's never coming home…'

Ellie pulled the blanket tighter around them.

'Listen, Jess, there was a girl back in my village. The day she found out her husband had been killed in action she never stopped smiling. It was the best thing that had ever happened to her. When he had a drink in him he'd beat her black and blue then he'd force himself on her. A month later she stopped her smiling. She'd had another letter. They'd made a mistake, got the name wrong. Her husband was alive and on his way home.'

Mistakes did happen; she'd read about them in the papers.

'I'll look after you, Jess, hold your hand and everything, that's what I used to do for my mother and I'll do the same for you. Nothing to it, a bit of pushing, a bit of shoving, and out it comes. Give your Tom something to look forward to. A trouble shared is a trouble halved. So, what do you say?'

FORTY-FIVE

April 1918

ALL SHE WANTED TO do was scream. If she did, the Major and his wife would hear her. They would run up the stairs and along the corridor into her attic bedroom. They would see Jess lying on the floor, her nightdress hitched over her hips, with Ellie kneeling beside her. They would call for the doctor and there would be hot water and clean sheets.

But screaming would also mean having her baby dragged out of her arms, lying there, helplessly, while it was handed over to a stranger – never being allowed to see her child again.

Ellie pushed a bundle of rags into her mouth.

'Here, bite on this.'

The Major and his wife had said nothing when, at six o'clock that evening, she'd told them that she was feeling ill and could she please have their permission to go upstairs to bed. The Major's wife had tilted her head to one side.

'What exactly is the problem?'

If they didn't hurry up, the baby, and everything else, all the blood and bits, would squeeze themselves out, down here in the living room, onto the Major's precious Indian silk carpet.

'It's…'

She indicated down below. Let the Major's wife think it was her monthly.

'I need to… lie down.'

She stood there, eyes down, back straight, her hands clenched into fists, as the pain knifed through her.

'Are you sure, Jess, that is all it is?'

All the Major's wife had to do was count back, the days, weeks and months, to when Tom was at home. But perhaps she'd already done that.

She bobbed a curtsey.

'Yes, ma'am.'

'You don't need a doctor?'

The Major looked her up and down over the top of his newspaper.

'No, sir.'

'Are you sure? If you do, you should say.'

'Yes, sir. Thank you, sir.'

She curtseyed again. But she wouldn't be able to do a fourth. Her legs would give way underneath her.

'Very well. You may go upstairs.'

Nothing to it, a bit of pushing, a bit of shoving and out it comes was how Ellie had described it. But then Ellie had never had a baby.

The pain was so awful she didn't think she would be able to get through the next two hours, let alone three or four, upstairs, alone in her room, with no one to hold her hand and no one to talk to. And Ellie had promised, when it happened, day or night, she would be there.

She'd used the excuse that a letter had been wrongly delivered to go round to the neighbouring house. She'd rung the bell and banged on the door, again and again, until after the third knock the door had opened.

She collapsed down onto her knees.

'What the…'

Ellie knelt down beside her.

'It's the baby. It's coming…'

'It's early…'

'Two weeks…'

'When did it start?'

'This morning…'

'What did you tell them?'

'That it was my monthly and I had to lie down…'

Ellie helped Jess up.

'I'll do the same. Go on now, back to the house, up to your room before someone sees us.'

Maids-of-all-work, crouched down together on the front door steps, whispering, could only mean one thing – trouble.

'Go on, I'll be as quick as I can.'

She'd crawled up the stairs to her bedroom. Her legs were shaking, her teeth were chattering, and the dull ache in her lower back was no longer a dull ache but pain so great it felt as if every bone in her body was being slowly and systematically crushed.

It had started that morning just after breakfast. She was completely unprepared when, out in the garden, hoeing the soil, ready for sowing seeds, she had felt a pop deep down in her stomach. Seconds later, warm liquid had gushed down the inside of her legs, soaking through the coarse brown skirt of her working dress.

The Major went on pacing up and down, marking out where the carrots, cabbages and swede should be sowed, while she continued on with the hoeing. It was a warm, sunny morning, the beginning of spring, and the liquid had dried quickly – something that only she could feel, and no one else could see, just like the baby turning inside her belly.

Her mother's waters had broken when they had been out together picking blackberries. Jess remembered her saying that there was nothing to be frightened about, that her brother or sister was now on his or her way. Nine hours later, the village midwife had called the two of them, her father and herself, into the cottage and there was her mother, propped up in bed, cradling a baby.

What she had tried to forget, but couldn't forget now, up

there in the attic, eleven hours into her own labour, was the sound of her mother screaming. It was like listening to an animal being ripped to pieces.

'Jess, you've just got to get the baby round the bend. Push down, really hard, like you want to go to the toilet. Come on, now, push...'

Women died in childbirth, she knew that. She had seen it in their village. One day there was a mother, father, and two kids, and the next day, there was just a father and two kids. Mother and baby had died in childbirth. These things happened.

'You're nearly there, girl, just push...'

It came in another wave, washing through her and over her. She sank underneath it, helpless, unable to breathe, suffocating in it, while her body expanded wider and wider, splitting further and further apart. She was no longer needed. It didn't matter what she thought, what she wanted, every muscle in her body was doing what it wanted to do, what it needed to do.

The pain became solid, more focussed.

'Jess, I can see it, the baby, just one big push...'

She pushed. There, sticking out between her legs was the head. She pushed. Her lower body convulsed and widened. Shoulders appeared, then arms, and what had been inside her, was now outside her.

FORTY-SIX

JESS FOLLOWED ELLIE DOWN the narrow flight of stairs.
Just less than nine months ago, she had crept down the same
staircase and along the landing into Tom's bedroom. When
she pushed open the door there he was waiting for her. That
was their last night together. And now here she was carrying
their child, less than two hours old, wrapped in a blanket in
her arms.

The door of the Major's bedroom opened. Snores echoed
up through the house. A floorboard creaked. Jess scrambled
underneath the tapestry-covered table. Ellie darted through
the door into the toilet. There was a shuffle of slippered feet
on the landing carpet. And then silence. There was another
shuffle. Jess peeped out. She could see her mistress; she was
standing at the top of the staircase, directly in front of where
Jess was hiding, looking down towards the hall below. She
turned towards the bedroom. The door closed.

Almost immediately, the door opened and the Major's
wife stepped back out onto the landing. She started to walk
towards the toilet. Jess closed her eyes. Please, no, don't let her
go in and find Ellie.

The footsteps stopped. There was a creak and a sigh and
then the shuffling came back down the landing, past where Jess
sat, crouched down on the floor, below the table. She tightened
her arms around the bundle of blanket containing her baby. The
footsteps stopped and then started up again, down the landing,
towards the bedroom. The door closed. Silence.

Jess opened her eyes. She crawled out from underneath the table. The toilet door opened and Ellie stepped out. They stood there, white faced, staring at each other. Together they went down the stairs, step by step, to the half-landing, and then down the final flight of stairs into the hallway. They pulled back the first bolt, then the second.

'When you go back up be careful…'

Ellie rolled her eyes.

'Jessica Brown, it was you not being careful that got us into this mess. And it will be me, Eleanor Baxter, who will get us out of it. Go on, hop it. Better wear out shoes than sheets.'

The front door clicked shut.

Keeping to the shadows, every few seconds glancing up at the sky, Jess followed the same route she and the Major had walked, marched, almost a year ago, when he collected her from the station that first day in London. Past the bombed out school where eighteen children had died and more than a hundred injured, down Glebe Road, Hillier Road, Honeywell Road, Ebbs Road.

Back in the village, when Jess and her mother had helped her father and the other men bring in the harvest, a full moon in a cloudless sky had been something to be welcomed, even celebrated; it would give them enough light to work on into the night. But in the city, in time of war, a full moon, like the one shining above, was something to dread.

Anti-aircraft fire started just as she was approaching the station. They were easy targets. All the enemy planes had to do was follow the tracks, shining in the moonlight, up the coast to London. If this one took a direct hit none of the people here, an old lady trying to comfort a whimpering dog, the little girl humming to a yellow bird in a cage, a mother watching over a sleeping child, would have a chance. What had made them all come to the station? They would have been safer staying at home.

Her ticket was checked. She'd been careful with the money. But, day by day, month by month, with every letter she'd written, and with every stamp she'd bought, it had disappeared. Buying her return ticket had all but emptied her purse. All that was left of the five pounds Tom had given her were two pennies and one sixpence.

The last train out from London to Lewes was leaving in two minutes. She had to catch it. Going back to the house with the baby wasn't an option. A child screamed, a man kicked, a woman cursed as Jess walked through, round and over the sleeping bodies, bunched up in blankets, carpeting the tunnel floor. Flights of steps led up from the tunnel onto the platforms; eight and nine, ten and eleven, twelve and thirteen.

She saw it, the hospital train, just before she reached the top of the steps. The doors were open and the wounded, and the dead and the dying, were being unloaded. Men in military uniform and nurses, white caps on their heads, red and grey capes covering their shoulders, walked up and down, whispering instructions. One stretcher was directed here, another there, another was loaded onto a truck parked at the side of the platform. There must have been hundreds of them.

A young woman, wearing a blouse, skirt and coat rather than a nurse's uniform, was walking down the platform towards where Jess was standing. Head down, looking from side to side, she checked each stretcher, before moving on, down the row, to the next, and the next, searching the battered and bloody remains for the one face she wanted to see.

There was a cry. The woman walked on. The cry was repeated. The woman stopped and turned. Jess had never seen Arthur Crow, the doctor's son, when he came back home from France. She'd only heard about him. How the children when they saw him, walking down the street, had screamed and run away. Now she understood why.

A young man was struggling to sit up. Or what was left of a young man. Where there should have been an arm and a hand with five fingers there was splintered bone. Where there should have been a leg and a foot with five toes there was a stump. On the right side of his head, instead of an ear and eye, there was a gaping hole.

The woman took a step back. She twisted from side to side, once, twice. She opened her mouth. Jess waited for the scream, for the young woman to pick up her skirts and run away. But instead the woman closed her mouth. She took one step forward, a second and then she ran towards the young man lying there on the ground. She knelt down beside him and took his hands in her hands.

Doors slammed shut. A whistle blew. The train pulled out of the station. Jess sat, looking out of the window, as it rattled southwards through the suburbs of Balham and Croydon. Two planes, one small, one twice its size, were caught silhouetted against the moon. The larger went into a steep dive, spinning round and round, down and down, towards the ground, fire flickering along the length of its fuselage.

FORTY-SEVEN

THE GRAVESTONES LINING THE path, leading up to the church, were so old and covered in moss that it was impossible to tell who they were remembering. But at least they were being remembered. Her brother had been buried in an unmarked grave. And the vicar had told her, in the letter Jess had received after her mother's death, that she too had been buried in the same churchyard, also in an unmarked grave. The poor got a hole in the ground but nothing else. Her mother had been lucky, given she had taken her own life, to get even that.

She tried the door, it was locked, but the night was dry and the porch would be a safe enough place to leave a baby until one of the wardens came up from the village to open the church. She sank down on to the stone floor and unbuttoned her dress. All she wanted to do was close her eyes and go to sleep but she couldn't. She had to finish feeding the baby then walk back up the river to Lewes to catch the first train into London.

She laid her daughter, wrapped in the blanket, down on the stone floor of the porch. She stood, buttoned up her dress, buttoned up her coat and then walked out into the churchyard – and kept on walking. If she hesitated for one single second, she wouldn't be able to do what she had to do. She hesitated. She took one step, then another and stopped. It was impossible.

She walked back up the path, past the rows of gravestones, to the porch. She picked up the bundle of blanket. She couldn't leave her daughter here. With food and coal so expensive and in such short supply, no one with a family of their own would want to take in an abandoned child. She would be sent off, to die, in the nearest orphanage.

Out of the churchyard, back through the village and down the lane towards the river; if her mother could do it, then she could too. She climbed up the steps. On her left, the river tumbled down a weir. To her right it flowed, slow and smooth, towards the sea. All she had to do was jump. The end would be fast – and painless.

Her own mother had starved herself so that Jess and her baby brother could have food. When she sent Jess off to London, she had believed that she would be saving her, making her safe, so that one day, like her mother before her, Jess would fall in love, get married and start her own family.

Jess could see her climbing up the steps onto the bridge, dressed in her black dress, her head covered in a shawl, the wind and the rain gusting around her. She closed her eyes and raised her arms. The wind whipped the shawl away from her body but her mother didn't move. She stood there, whispering a prayer, as the rain streamed down her face and over her shoulders. And then she dropped like a stone, her arms still outstretched, over the wooden railing, down into the river below.

And now she could see her father. He was one in a line of hundreds of soldiers, gas masks on, bayonets at the ready, walking up a hill. The man to her father's right staggered and fell. Blood fountained out of his skull. Directly ahead, at the top of the hill, stretching to the left and to the right, unbroken, was a solid wall of barbed wire. The dead and the dying, trapped and unable to escape, hung from it. And still her father walked on, straight, never hesitating, towards the wire. Bullets ripped through his chest, one step, two steps, on he continued. More machine-gun fire. One last step and then he collapsed, down, onto the ground.

He had not given up, even when he was walking to his own death. He did not turn and run away. He'd stayed, marching on, side by side, with his colleagues. For her father it had been the right thing, the only thing, to do.

And, standing alone together, up there on the Downs, he'd asked her to make him a promise – that however bad things were she would never give up. If she threw herself off the bridge, her daughter in her arms, she would be breaking that promise. Her father hadn't had a choice.

She did. There was still a chance, however small, that Tom was still alive and that, one day, he would come home. Killing herself, killing her baby, destroying his and his daughter's chance of happiness, would be mocking the sacrifices both her mother and father had made. She had to protect the future.

Jess walked back along the bridge, down the steps, across the meadow and up the lane to the church. A light was flickering in the ground floor of a house. In London a light burning out into the darkness, even just a candle breaking the blackout, would have immediately attracted the attention of the police. But out here, in the country, far away from the raids, nobody would bother or care. But, even so, it was strange. Someone had either got up very early or had never gone to sleep.

A woman dressed in a grey dress, a black mourning band on her right arm, was sitting at a table in the bay window. She was staring at a single candle, her right hand turning, and turning again, the gold wedding band on the fourth finger of her left hand. She was whispering what could only be a prayer. The woman hesitated. She looked out of the window. Jess shrank back behind a tree. The woman returned to her prayers.

Jess opened the gate and walked up the path to the front door. She placed her daughter down on the step. She unfastened the locket from around her own neck. She knelt down and slipped the locket round her daughter's.

It was almost exactly a year ago that Jess and her mother had buried her baby brother in the village churchyard. Her mother had thrown a bunch of primroses onto the tiny, white coffin lying there in its waterlogged grave. And now Jess was a mother and she, too, was saying goodbye to her child. She picked a single primrose from a bunch growing by the front door and slipped the flower underneath the blanket next to her daughter's heart.

'Goodbye, my love. Live well.'

Jess knocked on the front door. The woman paused but then went back to her prayers. Jess knocked again. The prayers stopped. The woman stood up. Jess ducked down behind a bush.

The door opened. The woman stood there, her shawl pulled tight around her shoulders, searching the darkness for the person who had knocked so loud and so long in the middle of the night. For a moment their eyes caught. There was whimper. The women looked down. The bundle of blanket sitting at her feet wriggled and squirmed.

'We'd always wanted children...'

The woman picked up the baby. She cradled it in her arms.

'Having a little boy, a little girl, a child of our own, would have been something to remember my husband by...'

There was no point in hiding. The woman knew she was there. Jess stepped out from behind the bush.

'You will look after her for me?'

The woman smiled.

'You're the girl from the market...'

The woman had seen Jess stealing her bread. She could have called out. The crowd would have heard and Jess would have been caught and handed over to the police. And tried as a thief.

'And you were in the churchyard, with your mother. You were there when I was visiting my husband's grave...'

The woman had recognised her, Jess had been certain of it, but she'd said nothing.

'We were burying my brother.'

The woman nodded.

'Your mother, is she–'

'She's dead.'

The woman nodded.

'I remember. There was talk of it in the village. And what about you... I'm sorry, I don't remember your name...'

A blackbird was singing its first song of the day.

'My name's Jess.'

She was running out of time.

'I'm a maid in London. I've got to get back...'

She ran out of the gate onto the track. The woman called after her.

'Does your daughter have a name?'

She'd worked so hard and so long to keep the baby a secret that she'd never thought about a name. It had seemed too much of a luxury.

'She's called...'

The scent, the tiny blue flowers, the needle-like leaves, the bush she'd been hiding behind was identical to one growing in her mother's garden. Her parents had planted it there, as a good omen for their marriage, on their wedding day.

'Her name's Rosemary. And you?'

'Martha. Martha Pearce.'

Jess ran down the track across the moonlit meadow. She ran over the bridge and then turned left to follow the riverside path back to the station and the first train into London.

FORTY-EIGHT

SAM OPENED HER EYES. The windowless, low-ceilinged intensive care unit, on the top floor of the hospital, had been replaced by a high-ceilinged, glass-walled, shiny-floored building which stretched on, up and down, in front and behind, to the left and right of her. The lights were on, the escalators whirring, the shops and restaurants bustling; she was in an air terminal and it was busy.

Soldiers, in dust-covered combat kit, huge rucksacks piled at their feet, stood together, talking, at one of the bars. Standing next to them, staring down into his beer, was a man dressed in head-to-toe black leather carrying a biker's helmet. An old lady, immaculately dressed in a pale pink suit, and carrying a white poodle, wandered past humming happily to herself. A group of women, dressed in black ankle-length robes, their heads covered, their children tagging along behind, eyes wide with curiosity, were being escorted through the terminal by two smartly dressed ground staff wearing blue trousers and matching blue jackets with a lapel badge featuring a pair of golden wings.

A couple, one very tall, the other very short, both with rucksacks on their backs and both wearing walking clothes and boots, stood staring up at the departure board. It had the usual flight departure times and flight numbers but instead of destinations, Paris, New York, Sydney, Milan, it listed the names of people. Against each name was a gate number. Some weren't yet open, some were delayed, others were boarding and some, George Thomas, Carol Maringa, Sai Thakar and Jennifer Robins, had already departed.

Her father's name was sixth on the list. His departure time was 1800 hours, his gate number was seventy-seven, and he was boarding. Sam checked her watch. It was 1750. "Flight Boarding" flicked to "Last Moments".

Behind and below the departure board was a large circular area. Leading off it were four corridors, each one clearly signposted. The first led to gates one to twenty, the second to gates twenty-one to forty, the third to gates forty-one to sixty and the fourth to gates sixty-one to eighty.

'Excuse me…'

An elderly man, bent low over a walking stick, was shuffling towards her. She didn't recognise the voice, she couldn't because she'd never heard it before, but she did recognise the grey face with the stubble and the staring eyes. It was Terry.

'Perhaps you'll be able to help me…'

He clamped a hand onto her arm.

'The lady told me I have to go to gate sixty-five. I'm sure that's what she said, I heard her quite clearly, gate sixty-five. But I can't find it anywhere. I've been going round and round for hours…'

She'd run away once. She couldn't do it again.

'Sixty-five's over there. It's on the way to where I'm going. I'll take you there.'

The old man's face lit up.

'Will you? How kind. Now where did I leave my bag? It's black and it's got my front door keys in it. I'll need them for when I get home, to let myself in. The place the social girl has put me in is lovely, they do all the cooking, all the washing, all the cleaning, just like a hotel, but it's just not the same. Not like being in your own home…'

There was no bag. And she couldn't remember seeing one beside the bed, in the old man's cubicle in the intensive care unit at the hospital.

The clock flipped to 1752.

'I think we should go to the gate. You don't want to miss your plane...'

She tugged him towards the corridor.

'My bag, I must have my bag. If don't have my bag, I won't have my keys and I won't be able to get in...'

'We'll ask at the gate...'

The old man stopped.

'I need to go to the toilet...'

1753.

'And when I have to go, I have to go, I can't hold on like I used to...'

'There'll be one on the plane...'

'Are you sure?'

'Yes. We're nearly there now. Just a couple of minutes...'

He shuffled forward.

'This is so exciting, such a surprise, I've never been in a plane before...'

They passed a businessman shouting at two airline staff.

'What do you mean there's no signal? I'm not getting on that plane until I've made the deal. Everything depends on it, everything...'

'I missed breakfast. Do they give you something to eat? A nice cup of tea and one of those French pastries, the flaky ones stuffed with chocolate...'

She put her hand underneath the old man's elbow, guiding him left round the refreshment stand.

'It depends on the length of the flight...'

At last they were at gate sixty-five.

'Will there be somebody there to meet me? My money's in my bag, I won't be able to pay for a taxi...'

'Please, Terry...'

He stopped. She tugged at his arm and then tugged again. The old man refused to move.

'Why does everyone keep calling me Terry? It makes me so angry. That sort of carelessness is so unnecessary. My name's…'

The clock flipped to 1754.

'My name's…'

The old man stamped his walking stick impatiently.

'My name's…'

They were standing at the top of a walkway that sloped down to the plane. Written on the side, to the left of the open door, was a name.

'Trevor, Trevor Jones. That's your name. Isn't it?'

'Yes, that's it, my dear. Of course it is. Trevor Jones. That's my name, how silly of me.'

A woman, dressed in blue trousers and jacket, stepped out of the plane. She was smiling. She was also carrying a black bag.

Sam turned and ran up the walkway and out into the main corridor. It was 1755. She had just five minutes until her father's departure time. She ran past gates sixty-six, sixty-seven, sixty-eight and sixty-nine. The clock flipped to 1756. The corridor narrowed, turned sharp left and stopped at a lift.

She pushed the call button and pushed again. There were no stairs, no escalator; the lift was the only way down. The doors creaked open. She stepped inside. The doors creaked closed. She punched the down button. The lift jolted, shuddered and then began to move. It jerked to a stop. The doors creaked open.

The clock flipped to 1757. And there was gate seventy-seven, just ahead. She pushed herself forward.

1758.

She ran down the ramp towards the plane. A name was written underneath the cockpit window. Sitting inside, talking to traffic control, was Michael Foster – her father. His plane was about to take off.

'Wait, please, wait. Open the door…'

She would never hear his voice.

'I must speak to him…'

She would never see his smile.

'Please let me speak to him.'

Never feel the warmth of his arms around her.

'Please help me.'

She hammered on the side of the plane with her fists.

'Let me in…'

And hammered again.

'Please let me in…'

The door remained shut. She collapsed down onto her knees.

'Please help me… whoever you are… if you're out there… please help me. Please help me save my father…'

There was silence and then a scrape of metal on metal. The door of the plane slid back. Long coat, lace-up boots, brown hair tied back in a ribbon, it was the girl Sam had followed to Tudor Close, the same girl who had been standing underneath the street lamp, on the opposite side of the road, outside the house.

She pulled Sam onto the plane.

'No questions, you've got one minute, that's all, before this plane goes…'

The cockpit door was immediately to her left. It was locked – ready for take-off.

'Dad, it's me, Sam.'

Nothing. She knocked again and, again, nothing; the metal door was too heavily reinforced.

'He can't hear me.'

Now she had only seconds. The girl was standing beside her.

'You've been on a plane, you've watched, you know what to do…'

The girl was right. She had flown many times and, if her father was one of the pilots, Sam and her mother were usually upgraded to first or business class. They would sit, in the front, hoping to get a quick wave from her father whenever someone went in or out of the cockpit. And on a long flight, when the cabin crew needed to open the door, to take her father and his first officer a meal, what did they do? The keypad, there it was, on the wall to the right of the door.

'There's a code, I need the code…'

'The only person who knows the code is you, Sam…'

'But I don't–'

'Think, Sam, think hard. In thirty seconds this door will close, this plane will push back and you won't be on it. They'll drag you off…'

The keyboard was made up of letters, not numbers, so the code could be either a sequence, without any particular order, or a word with some meaning: a name, a place or a thing. She punched in "DAD". The door remained bolted.

There were people outside, she could hear their voices. One of them was talking on a radio.

'What do you want most, Sam, for you and your father, right now?'

Try to be calm. Try to think.

'For him to be alive and well… to be safe?'

The girl smiled.

'Try it, Sam, punch it in.'

"SAFE". Nothing.

The plane juddered. Her father had told her about the gate agents and the dispatchers, the people responsible for getting the plane off on time.

'I don't know it…'

'You do, Sam, you do…'

She punched in "LOVE" because that's what she'd tell

him, when he opened the door, and she walked into the cockpit. That she loved him. Nothing.

A man, wearing a bright yellow plastic jerkin and carrying a clipboard, was walking towards her.

'Time's up.'

He took her arm.

'This plane's got to go.'

She reached out and with the tip of one finger punched in "HOME". Because that was what she wanted, most, right now; to be at home, the three of them together, a happy family in the house on the hill overlooking the sea.

FORTY-NINE

'MY MOTHER HAD ME when she was fifteen, same age as I am now, but her parents wouldn't let her keep me. They took me away, put me up for adoption...'

Amy looked so small, so vulnerable, sitting up in the hospital bed, her week-old baby sucking at her breast.

'I thought my mum and dad would do the same, so I didn't tell them, I kept it a secret. It was stupid, dangerous, not just for me, but for her. My mum and dad were more upset than angry, not about me having the baby, but because I hadn't told them.'

'Didn't they guess?'

Amy shrugged.

'I lied, all the time, tons of them, like I was allergic to wheat, which was why my tummy was so big. And I had a skin disease, which was why I had to wear leggings and baggy jumpers and t-shirts, even in the summer, on the beach with my friends, when it was really hot. Everybody believed me, everybody, my friends, my teachers, even my parents. I wouldn't. But they all did...'

The baby burped, blinked and then closed her eyes. The last time Sam had seen her was six days ago in the special baby unit.

'I tried not to think about it, having her, just hoped it would be quick, that it wouldn't hurt...'

'Did it?'

'What?'

'Did it hurt?'

'Are you stupid or something? Of course, it hurt. It's like there's a rat in your stomach, eating you, and the rat just keeps getting bigger and hungrier, until there's nothing left of you except the worse pain ever…'

Alone, nobody there to hold her hand; trying not to scream out because she didn't want to wake her parents.

'A friend, somebody, there's no way I could have done it on my own …'

'You do what you have to do…'

Amy shrugged.

'I cleaned myself up, got dressed, wrapped her in a towel and put her in the bag. My parents keep loads of old stuff so that was easy to sort. It was still dark, must have been early, like seven or eight, something like that. It was raining but I made sure she was warm and dry, and we got downstairs and out of the house without waking them. I didn't know what I was doing, where I was going, I just caught the bus, saw the hospital, got off and left her in the car park. I phoned to tell them. I went back later, in the afternoon, to make sure she wasn't still there…'

The same day, Sunday, her father had been admitted.

'You were wearing the jacket, with the flash on the sleeve, the one I saw in your bedroom. It was Sunday, my mother had just arrived at the hospital, I went to the toilet and you came out of a cubicle and you were crying…'

'I was pretty desperate…'

How desperate, so desperate, she'd try to kill herself? The timing, everything, was exactly right.

'Amy, my dad, a girl walked out in front of his car, he had to brake, hard, and that's when he knocked his head. The girl wasn't hurt. She ran away. But my father nearly died. Was that you? Did you walk out in front of my father's car?

Amy flushed.

213

'What are you saying? That I tried to top myself?'

'You said you were desperate, didn't know what you were doing...'

'If I did want to top myself I wouldn't do something as boring as walk out in front of your dad's car. I'd swig back a bottle of vodka, and then chuck myself off the end–'

'Sam, it is Sam, isn't it?'

A woman was walking towards the bed. Following her was a man carrying a very large, very pink teddy bear.

'Amy's been going on and on about you. We're Ann and Malcolm...'

Sam stood up.

'You'll come and see us, won't you?'

Amy looked up.

'Yeh, we'd love to see you, both of us, me and little Sam. Couldn't call her anything else could I? And you could do a bit of nappy changing, get your hand in, for when you have one of your own...'

No way.

'And, Sam, the postcard, the one with the blue sea and white beach, how me and mum and dad, how we'd all be going back...'

'You'd closed your eyes, I thought you were going to die, but that's when you opened your eyes. It must have been very special...'

Amy laughed.

'The blue sea and the white beach? There's no such place. I faked it, the card, made it up on the Internet.'

FIFTY

'THANK YOU, DAD.'

His smile was a bit crooked and his face a bit puffy, but her father didn't look bad for someone who'd just come back from the dead.

'Thank you, Mum.'

She hugged and kissed her mother.

'I've got you another present.'

Her mother pulled a tissue-wrapped parcel from her handbag.

'It started with my great-grandmother, and it's come down, all the way through the family, mother to daughter, mother to daughter, and now it's my turn to give it to you.'

It was square and hard.

'Dad bought me the box. What matters is inside…'

The door opened. Mac walked into the room.

'Bringing your father back from the dead, that, Sam Foster, is a result. But now we need to make sure that the miraculous recovery continues.'

He placed a beaker on the bedside table.

'Mr. Foster, the sooner you take your pills, the sooner you'll be back flying your planes…'

'I'm not doing any more flying.'

A few minutes before the room had been full of laughter. Now it was full of the worst possible silence.

'But Mr. Foster, there's no reason why you–'

'Nothing to discuss.'

Sam darted a look across at her mother. Did she know about this?

Her father leant his head back against the pillow.

'Time to get grounded.'

He closed his eyes.

'Dad…'

Sam threw herself onto the bed.

'But the planes, you love them…'

He opened his eyes.

'Hey, what's all this…'

'Flying, that's what you do, that's who you–'

He hugged her tight.

'I can live without the planes. But I can't live without you. And I most certainly can't live without your mother…'

Her parents were giving each other one of those looks.

'Now it's time for you two to go home. We'll talk later. After you've opened your last present…'

'Come on, Sam. There's this new recipe…'

Her mother was pushing her towards the door.

'A Spanish stew. I've got some fish in the freezer and I thought we could use that. You fry some onion and potatoes and then you add garlic, some paprika and some cayenne–'

'Dad…'

She had to ask.

'The girl, the one who walked out in front of your car, can you remember what she looked like?'

Her father picked up the beaker.

'Short, reddish blonde hair, leggings and a jacket…'

Her father gulped down the pills.

'With a red, blue and silver flash on the sleeve.'

She had been right. It was Amy.

'Did she do it on purpose? Did she see you coming? Or was it a mistake, like she was really upset, crying, didn't see you–'

'Sam, what's this all about? Your father needs to rest...'

'It's important, Mum.'

Her father nodded.

'OK, I was driving down the street. The girl was walking towards me. Her head was down. Her shoulders were hunched. She looked upset. Perhaps she was crying. I don't know for certain. I didn't think much of it. It was Sunday, early in the morning, and I thought she must have had a row, perhaps with her parents, but more likely a boyfriend. I was about to pass her when she suddenly, without any warning, without looking up to check, turned and walked out between two parked cars into the road. The rest you know.'

She sank down on the chair beside her father's bed.

'Does that answer your question?'

She had to know.

'The girl didn't look up, but she might have heard you, known you were there...'

'That's true. Sam, why is this so important to you...'

'You could have died. If the girl did it on purpose, knew what she was doing–'

Mac put his hand on her shoulder.

'Sam, this girl, do you know who she is?'

Did it matter whether Amy did or didn't walk out in front of her father's car? It was a small detail that had been important at the time but, perhaps, not now. If she confronted Amy, insisting on the truth, her foster parents would find out that she had tried to kill herself. It would only cause unhappiness.

It was the big scheme that mattered. Not the detail. Her father was alive and well and coming home to live with Sam and her mother. And Amy and her baby were alive and going home to live with her foster parents.

She looked up at Mac. He looked back at her.

'Sam?'

Decision made.

'No. I don't.'

They all had a future. Even if that future meant having to change nappies…

FIFTY-ONE

April 7th 1918

THERE WAS A WHISTLE, a belch and the train pulled out of the station. It was difficult to believe that just over six hours ago she had been standing here, on the same platform, cradling her newborn baby in her arms. There were no doctors, no nurses, no stretchers, no moans or screams. The hospital train had vanished along with its cargo.

She ran down the stairs into the tunnel. The little girl was humming. The yellow bird was singing. The mother was rolling up her blanket. The dog was wagging its tail. And instead of the kicking and the cursing there was chatter and laughter. The station hadn't taken a direct hit. The people who had spent the night sheltering within its walls were all still alive.

'German attacks fail at all points.'

Outside, on the station forecourt, a boy was selling newspapers.

'Amiens front stands firm.'

It was only April but she was sweating inside the itchy cocoon of her ankle-length coat. Jess stopped and raised her face up to the sun. Warmth and light replaced the cold and dark of the night she had been dreading, and which she had never expected to live through.

Taking Rosemary back to the village, where she had grown up, had been the right thing to do. Her daughter would be safe down there in the country with Martha looking after her. She would have food in her stomach, clean clothes on her back and there would be enough money to buy coal for a fire and medicine if she was sick. But don't let it be for too long. Because Jess wanted to be there at her daughter's side, holding her daughter's hand, as her own mother had held hers, when she took her first step. And there, cradling her on her lap, when she looked up, giggled, and spoke her first word.

With the Germans now on the run the war could be soon at an end. Tom would come back home to them, she was sure of it, and when he did she and little Rosemary would be waiting for him. Whether they would get married, whether she would ever be his wife, she didn't know. She could only wish, only hope, that their story, the one they'd started together, would have a happy ending.

There were two ways back to Eaton Villa. The first was the route the Major had taken the day she arrived in London; down Ebbs Road, left into Honeywell Road, right into Hillier Road and, finally, left into Glebe Road. She'd chosen to walk that way to the station, last night, as the roads were wide and safe. And the houses would have given some shelter if there had been an air raid. It was also the route that she and Ellie used when they went shopping together.

But if she followed the path along the side of the railway track, back towards the warehouses, and then took the shortcut down the lane, across the common, she would be able to take at least ten minutes off the journey. She would never have used it at night, it was just too dangerous. But it was six in the morning. Last night's drinking pals, any that were still around, would be too far gone to make themselves a nuisance.

Ellie would have tidied up her bedroom and cleared all trace of what had happened there the night before. But she had to be back at the house in time to light the range, heat up the water and take up the Major and his wife their morning tea. If she didn't, they would go upstairs to her room. And find it empty.

She followed the narrow footpath, squeezed between a wire fence and a high, brick wall, back along the railway tracks in the same direction her train had just come from.

A low, insistent drumming grew steadily louder and nearer. A dull thump and the ground beneath her feet rocked and heaved. There was another thump. And now the drumming was no longer background, but foreground, drilling its way into every bone and sinew in her body. Up ahead, flying towards her out of the early morning sun, was a plane. A huge ball of fire billowed up into the sky.

The footpath opened out into a yard between two derelict warehouses. Out here, if the plane dropped a bomb, she would be killed. She had to get inside. She ran towards the nearest warehouse. She pushed on the door. It stayed closed. She threw herself at the door. It refused to move. She tried one more time. Metal clanked down onto concrete. The door opened.

She was in a hallway. In front of her was a staircase lit by a single window. She would be safer on the ground floor. And she would be safer further inside. To her right was a set of double doors. She pushed. They opened easily. The main storage area of the warehouse was empty but instead of being dark, which was what she had been expecting, it was light.

The memory she cherished most was the last few moments she and her father had spent together. She had nursed it, keeping it alive inside her head; walking out of the door of the cottage, through the garden and onto the track, climbing up the hill, side by side, her hand in his hand, onto the top of the ridge.

Her father stepping forward and putting his arms around her and the hoping, the longing, that she would never ever have to step out of them. That they could stay that way, father and daughter, daughter and father, up there on top of the world, together for ever. And then the low, insistent drumming, getting steadily louder and nearer, and there, without any warning, swooping down on them out of the sky, the white plane with black crosses on the underside of its wings.

And there it was now. Right there directly above her. She could see it through the glass roof of the warehouse: the same white plane with the same black crosses on the underside of its wings.

FIFTY-TWO

Eaton Villa, London, SW11

April 6th, 1934

Dear Jess

I'm writing this letter on the day of our daughter's 16th birthday. I've tried before, so often, more times than I can remember, but every time I sat down and started to write the words refused to come. But today feels different. The words are coming, and more than coming – they are writing themselves.

I'm not sure where to start but I think it has to be with the letter you wrote telling me that you were expecting our child. I did get it. And I was going to write back to you. And to my parents, telling them about the baby, and asking them to look after the both of you until I returned from France and could, as soon as you reached sixteen, make you my wife. I knew it would be a terrible shock to them, my father's hopes of who I would marry, where I would eventually find my place in society, had always been high, too high, since the loss of my two brothers. But I also knew that they would have done what I was asking of them. But I was never allowed to write that letter because within a day of receiving it I had been taken prisoner.

When our trench was overrun and my men and I were being marched back away from the battlefield, a shameful joy swept through me. I wasn't going to die the terrible death I had seen so many other men die. I would be taken to an official prisoner of war camp where I would be formally registered as a POW. Word would be sent back to you and my parents, through the Red Cross, that I was alive and well. And then all I would have to do was keep my head down, keep my mouth closed and wait out the war. And then come back home to you.

But none of that happened. I was never registered, my name was never given to the Red Cross, and I was never sent to an official POW camp. Instead, I became one of the nameless missing, kept in France and forced to work in a prisoner of war labour company delivering shells and digging trenches just behind the front line. I watched, helpless, as the men around me died. Dying would be easy. It was the staying alive that was going to be difficult.

I could have insisted that as an officer, exempt from hard labour by international law, I should be removed from the front line and taken to the safety of a camp. But leaving my men there, almost certainly facing certain death, from being beaten and starved, or blown to pieces by their own country's guns, was unthinkable. I could not do it.

We worked twelve sometimes sixteen hours a day, without a break, seven days a week. The building in which we were housed had no roof. There were no beds and no blankets. We wore, week after week, month after month, the same clothes we had been captured in. We never took them off. We were given a single meal each day of a quarter of a loaf of black, lumpy bread, some watery turnip soup and lukewarm coffee made out of barley. The weight dropped off us. We became so weak that the march to the frontline became almost impossible but we had to do it, we didn't have a choice, because if we didn't it would mean even less food and even more beatings.

Civilians, when they saw us, tried to give us food. A woman threw me some bread when we were being marched through her village. We were both punished – I was beaten, she was shot. Another time, it wasn't the civilian that was shot, but one of my own men.

It wasn't hard to hate those who were guarding us – the enemy. And it is so easy to see how this hatred starts, and how that hatred spreads. It is not so easy to forgive. But you must. That is the only way to get through – the only way to survive. The men who were guarding us were not so different. They, too, were sons, brothers and husbands. And they, too, had little enough food themselves. Their families back at home even less.

There was much talk at the battlefront about the dead coming back to protect the living; angels striding out towards the enemy lines, everyone seemed to have seen one or heard of one. But I always regarded the stories as nothing but superstitious nonsense. But if it gave the men comfort, and they needed comforting given that most of them were going to die out there on the front line, then, it did no harm – who was I to laugh or complain. That's what I believed – until, one day, I saw my own angel.

It was April 7th, 1918. The guards had kicked us awake at four in the morning. We'd eaten our crust of bread, drunk our sip of water, and now we were being marched out of camp. It must have been about six o'clock but if the sun was rising we couldn't see it. Day didn't exist on the front line, only night. And that's when the shell hit us.

One minute I was walking, the next I was laying there, face down, in a sludge of blood and bone. I hurt so much that all I wanted to do was die. And that's when I saw my angel. And the angel I saw was you – my Jess. You didn't have wings, and you didn't have a halo. Nor were you sounding your trumpet. For which I was grateful. You were just standing there, buttoned up in your coat, your hair tied back and your face flushed as if you'd been running. And you looked just like you. But at the same time you didn't. There was something different; you looked as though you were lit up from inside. You were, quite literally, glowing. And everything that I had always found beautiful, the green of your eyes, the whiteness of your skin, was even more pronounced – and even more beautiful. And you looked so happy.

I don't remember saying anything, I don't think I could, but if I did it was just your name. But that wasn't important, any other words would have just got in the way, because, in those few seconds, I've never felt closer to you. And then, and I'm searching here for the right word, you faded.

You were gone and I was left lying there, and that's when I made the decision to stand up and walk rather than lie there and die. And that was exactly what I did, although quite quickly the standing up and walking turned into a very painful and very undignified crawling which lasted through the whole of that day, into the night, and then on into the next day when I finally fell, head first, down into a trench on the Allied lines.

My next memory is waking up in hospital in France. Two weeks later I was sent back home to England. And you weren't there. My parents explained that, just before serving dinner, you had complained of feeling unwell. They had offered to send out for a doctor but you had said it was unnecessary; if you could go and get some rest you would be fine in the morning. They ate the dinner that you had prepared for them and then went upstairs to bed. In the morning, when you failed to appear with their tea, they went up to your room. There was no one there.

When I arrived home you had been reported missing for over two weeks. Nobody cared, nobody was interested and most certainly not the police; you were just another girl, who'd got herself into trouble. Good riddance to bad rubbish.

It was your friend Ellie, the maid next-door, who told us that you'd given birth to a little girl and that you had left the house around midnight to take her back to your village. And that's where I found her.

When Martha described you to me, told me what had happened, the knocking on the door, the baby on the doorstep, I knew that the Jess she described had been you and that the baby was our daughter. Your locket, the one I had given you just before I left for France, fastened round Rosemary's neck, confirmed that.

But where were you? I already knew but I was avoiding it. I was still hoping that what I had seen so clearly had been nothing more than a hallucination and that you were alive and well, and that I would, eventually, be able to find you. But, in my heart, I knew I was fooling myself; you had gone to a place where I would never be able to reach you.

Two months later there was a knock on the door. It was the police. A body of a girl, answering your description, had been found under the bombed out remains of a disused warehouse. The warehouse had taken a direct hit around six o'clock on the morning of April 7th – the time of my hallucination. There was not much to go on – some scraps of clothing, a purse containing a return train ticket to Lewes, and a few strands of hair – but that was enough: enough, at least, to convince someone who already knew.

Our daughter remained with Martha living down in the country. To split them up would have been too heartbreaking. I go down to see them whenever I can, which is often. And Rosemary comes up here to stay in London. Now that she's sixteen, I think, I hope, that her visits will be far more frequent.

My mother and father died two years ago, within two months of each other. You asked me, that first evening down in the kitchen, whether your mother had gone to hell because she had committed suicide. And I said, no, it's the people left behind, who did nothing to help, who will spend the rest of their lives in hell – a hell, in this present life, of their own making. And that was what happened to both my parents.

My mother told me, confessed to me, just hours before she died, that when she found out you were pregnant, and that I was the father, instead of helping you she threatened you, saying that if she told my father he would have you thrown out of the house.

What she didn't know was that my father already knew what had happened between us. I told him, privately, the morning I left to return to France. To say that he was less than happy would be an understatement. But he promised that whatever happened, whether I did or did not return from France, you would always be looked after. And, for all his faults, my father was a man who always kept his word.

If my mother had talked to my father, and my father had talked to my mother, there would have been a wedding, rather than a funeral, on my return from France.

Eaton Villa is far too large for me alone. But it is where we spent the little time we had together, and it is where our daughter was born, so this is where I stay. I can't imagine living anywhere else. A very capable housekeeper looks after both myself and the house – your friend and companion, Ellie.

You were fifteen when we met and you were still fifteen when you gave birth to our daughter. And she is, as of today, already older than you. Whenever she walks into the room, and I look up, it is you I see. When she takes my hand it is you who is taking my hand. And when she laughs it is you who is laughing. She is so like you – in every way.

I know that you won't, physically, be able to read this letter, but in putting these words down I hope that somehow it will bring me nearer to you, that you will be able to hear and feel and understand how much you are missed and how much you were loved – and are still loved. And always will be loved.

You are and always will be my angel.

Your loving Tom.

FIFTY-THREE

SAM READ TOM'S LETTER not once, not twice but three times, each word again, again and again. There was a sheet of thick, plain paper, folded in half, in the same envelope. She opened it. 'Jess' was written below a pencil sketch of a girl. Sam recognised her instantly.

There was a much smaller box inside the larger, elaborately carved Moroccan one her mother had given her. She slipped off the lid. A purple velvet cushion and, sitting on it, a heart-shaped locket on a chain.

There was a catch on the side. She pressed it. The locket opened. There were two compartments. The right hand one contained a dried flower, very brittle, very pale, but unmistakably a primrose. What it was doing there, why it was so important, she didn't know; there had been no mention of a primrose in Tom's letter. The left hand compartment contained a photograph, head and shoulders only, of a young man in military uniform.

"You are and always will be my angel."

That's what Tom had written at the end of his letter.

"You are and always will be my…"

Angel.

Sam picked up her jacket. She ran out of her bedroom, along the landing and down the stairs.

'Hello. Yes, she's here…'

Her mother held out the phone.

'It's your dad.'

'Hello, yes, look, Dad, I've got to go out...'

Her mother's fish stew was simmering, not boiling over, on top of the oven. Apples, bananas and pears were piled high in the blue and white ceramic bowl and lilies, pink ones with orange spots, were sitting in a glass vase on top of the bookcase.

'Yes, I've read it, yes, the letter. Look, Dad, can I call you later, when I get back? Yes, I promise...'

She held out the mobile.

'Sam, what's the matter? Is something wrong?'

The box, the letter, the photographs inside the locket, Jess and Tom, it was all too complicated to explain. And her mother would never believe her.

'Supper will be ready soon.'

'I won't be long.'

'But where are you going?'

'To see some friends...'

Sam ran out of the kitchen into the hallway.

'Hello, yes. I don't know. Some friends. Yes, that's what she said. The girls I expect, Katie, Lou and Shelly. It is her birthday...'

She pulled open the front door and ran down the hill, across the road and onto the promenade. The moon rode high in the night sky. A seagull shrieked overhead.

Poppy wreaths were laid out in rows, in front of a plaque, just above the base of the angel statue.

"Our loved ones have departed and we ne'er shall see them more,
Till we meet before the pure and crystal sea
Till we clasp the hands we loved so well upon the golden shore
What a meeting, what a meeting that will be!"

For a moment, the waves rolling off into the far distance seemed to solidify, their peaks and troughs changing into the ridges and hollows of a sea of mud rather than of a sea of water.

Almost instantly the sea transformed itself back, the mud once again reverting to water.

'May I introduce you...'

He had been standing underneath the statue exactly a week ago. He had turned and smiled as she walked past on her way home from the fairground.

"To the Angel of Peace."

The young man, dressed in khaki breeches, knee-high leather boots, a wide belt with a strap going over his right shoulder, gestured to the statue. Wings outstretched against the sky, right hand clutching an olive branch, it towered above them.

'Out in France, I thought my men were crazy. They were always talking about angels, but then I saw one. She didn't have wings nor was she carrying an olive branch...'

'Not that olive branches work...'

Sam twirled round. Ankle-length coat, lace-up boots: it was Jess.

'That statue was put there in 1912. Six years later, nineteen million people had died in the so-called war to end all wars...'

'I can see you. I can hear you. You and Tom...'

The clock striking five o'clock in a house where there was no such clock. The fair, being on the ghost train, going through those doors and instead of sitting in the cab next to Leo, she was standing on a platform, of a station, watching stretchers being unloaded off a train. Standing out on the balcony, waiting for the fireworks to start, the flash of white light and then seeing the sea of mud. The deep boom reverberating up towards the sky, the air shuddering, and then the road, the houses, the cars, all disappearing, just as if a bomb had fallen out of the sky.

'But why, why did you show me all those things...'

'Only you, Sam, nobody else, not even me and Tom, could follow your father and bring him back.'

'But you were there, in the plane, you opened the door. You helped me…'

'Only when you asked…'

They were standing on either side of her. Jess on her left. Tom on her right.

'But, first you had to do what Jess and I have had to do…'

A memory was nudging at her. It was years ago. It was night and she was lying curled up under the duvet, eyes tight shut, alone in her room, listening to the very large, very angry giants rumbling up and down overhead. There were solid walls above, underneath and all around her. But that wouldn't stop them. Nothing could stop them, not even her parents, if the giants wanted to come and get her.

'Sam.'

A voice whispered her name.

'Come out now, don't be afraid.'

The duvet was tugged back. She opened her eyes. The young woman took her left hand. The young man took her right hand. They led her, across the room, over to the window. The man lifted her up onto a stool. The woman pushed back the curtains. Lightning forked, thunder rolled, wind howled and rain lashed. But there were no giants.

'You had to face your fear.'

'It was you – you and Tom – you were my invisible friends. And when mum made us move, to this house, you went away…'

'If you want Jess and I to go–'

'No.'

Sam pulled the locket out of her jacket pocket.

'I want you to stay.'

Jess' fingers were soft. Her breathe was warm. She fastened the locket around Sam's neck.

'Happy birthday, Sam.'

Sunshine flooded into the cottage through the open door. Lambs skipped and jumped on the Downs, starlings were nesting in the thatch below the chimney and bumblebees were buzzing in and out of the blackthorn. Soon it would be warm enough to eat outside. Along paths, up lanes and over hills, wherever they ended up, sitting on top of Highdown Hill, her father telling her stories about the people who had lived there thousands of years before, or on Burrow Head watching the peregrine falcons circling over the white chalk cliffs, or in one of the valleys, the deans, hidden away below the Downs, he would always find a perfect place for a picnic.

But the memory she cherished most was the last few moments she and her father had spent together. She had nursed it, keeping it alive inside her head; walking out of the door of the cottage, through the garden and onto the track, climbing up the hill, side by side, her hand in his hand, and then stopping there on the ridge.

Her father stepping forward and putting his arms around her and the hoping, the longing, that she would never ever have to step out of them. That they could stay that way, father and daughter, daughter and father, up there on top of the world, together for ever. And then the low, insistent drumming, getting steadily louder and nearer. And there, without any warning, swooping down on them out of the sky: the white plane with black crosses on the underside of its wings.

And there it was now, right there, directly above her. She could see it through the glass roof of the warehouse; the same white plane with the same black crosses.

'Jess?'

It was her father's voice. She instantly recognised it and then just as instantly denied it. How could it be? He was dead. But there he was, exactly the way she remembered him. And standing behind him, cradling her baby brother in her arms, both of them plump-cheeked and laughing, was her mother.

He stepped forward and put his arms around her. She buried herself in his familiar warmth.

'We've come to take you home.'

234